SHEENA'S DILEMMA
It's Better To Marry Than To Burn

a novel by Reign

Dreams Books
Dreams Publishing Company
www.dreamspublishishing.com

Dreams Publishing Company
Post Office Box 4731
Rocky Mount, North Carolina 27803
www.DreamsPublishing.com

This book is a work of fiction. Names, characters, places, and incidents either are products of the author's imagination or are used fictitiously. Any resemblance to actual events or locales or persons, living or dead, is entirely coincidental.

© 2007 by Reign

All rights reserved. No part of this book may be reproduced, stored in a retrieval system, or transmitted in any form or by any means without the prior written consent of the Publisher. This book is sold subject to the condition that it shall not, by way of trade or otherwise, be lent, resold, hired out, or otherwise circulated without the publisher's prior consent in any form of binding or cover other than that in which it was published and without a similar condition including this condition being imposed on the subsequent publisher. If you purchased this book without a cover, you should be aware that this book is stolen property. It was reported as "unsold and destroyed" to the Publisher and neither the Author nor the Publisher has received any payment at all for this now called "Stripped Book."

Dreams Titles are available at special quantity discounts for bulk purchases for sales promotion, premiums, fund-raising, educational, or institutional use. Special book excerpts or customized printings can also be created to fit specific needs. For details, write to:

Dreams Publishing Company, Post Office Box 4731, Rocky Mount, North Carolina 27803; Attention: Special Sales.

Cover Designed by Nicki Angela
Models: Brittney Child and Jon Crudup
ISBN13: 9780978897703
ISBN: 0978897706

Library of Congress Control Number (LCCN): 2007932099
1. Family & Relationships – Love & Romance
2. African American Women – Fiction
3. Interpersonal Relationships

First Dreams Books Printing: February 2008
10 9 8 7 6 5 4 3 2 1

Manufactured in the United States of America

Proverbs 31:30

Favour is deceitful, and beauty is vain: but a woman that feareth the LORD, she shall be praised.

Proverbs 18:22

Whoso findeth a wife findeth a good thing, and obtaineth favour of the LORD.

Chapter One

Sheena Daniels rubbed her eyes before looking over at the clock that sat on the bookshelf in her office. It was almost quitting time, and this day couldn't be over soon enough.

She had been working for the United States Department of Education as an attorney since the year she graduated from law school. This is where she and Jason Jackson had come to know and love each other. He had worked in this same office up until a year ago. Now he worked out of the Atlanta office and she missed their Thursday night bowling practices, their intense games of Scrabble or Monopoly, their Friday night movie marathons, and she even missed arguing with him about politics.

Sheena wiped the tears from her eyes telling herself that better days were ahead, she just had to get through *this* day. She had cried more today than when Jason first told her on Sunday that he would no longer be seeing her. She turned her swivel chair to face the window. The weather on the outside was just as dreary as it was on the day their relationship took a turn for the worse. Just thinking about that day brought on a deep depression. They were supposed to be friends, the very best of friends, and that decision was made by the two of them. It was Jason who had changed his mind about their agreement. He didn't want to be just friends any more. He wanted to be her husband, her lover, father of her children, and now she felt betrayed. He had promised they would always be friends and he reneged on his word.

Though that conversation had taken place more than a year ago, she remembered it as if it were yesterday. Sheena could hardly speak after Jason told her he was in love with her. As the words came from his lips, she saw the sincerity in his eyes and knew he meant what he was saying. "I love you, Sheena. I can't help how I feel about you."

"But we agreed to be friends, Jason. We've discussed this, and we came to the same conclusion: that we should remain friends," she had told him.

"I don't want to be just your friend anymore," he protested.

"Why, Jason? Why have you changed your mind now? I don't understand. We agreed long ago to just be friends."

"I can't help how I feel about you. I can't help how my body reacts to you. I love you, Sheena. I've tried to tell myself we are just friends but my mind and my body just won't agree."

For a long time no one spoke. Then she turned to him. "So, what are we supposed to do? Just act as if the other doesn't exist?"

He walked over to where she stood. "I know a solution." He positioned himself directly in front of her.

"Which is?" she asked nervously.

"We can take it one step at a time. We're already the best of friends; we already do everything couples do. We just never had the romance. We can just add it as we…"

"No, Jason. I like things the way they are."

"Then, I guess it's settled." He moved away from her, heading toward the door. "I asked for a transfer and it's come through. I'm leaving." There was tremendous pain in his voice, and she could feel the tears pressing against the backs of her eyes.

"It doesn't have to be this way," she choked out.

"Yes, it does. I don't want… I can't be around you."

She physically jiggled herself to ward off the memory.

Sheena had been unable to concentrate on work today. The case she was writing an answer to should have only taken a few hours, not the entire day. She heard a tap on her door.

"Come in," she answered putting away her self pity for the moment.

Carol pushed the door open and leaned against the door jamb with her overcoat draped across her arm. "You're not pulling another late night, are you, Sheena?" Carol was the department's Administrative Assistant, ensuring that the Attorney's Division was run efficiently. But she was also nosey and knew everyone's business – something that wasn't too hard to do since most of the calls came through her.

"No," she answered using her thumb and index finger to rub her eyes as if they had been strained by the computer screen, when in fact; she was attempting to hide the truth about her red puffy eyes. "I'll only be here another half-hour or so. I'm meeting Marshall for dinner."

"Marshall?" Carol asked with curiosity.

"Yes, Vincent Marshall."

"Oh, are you talking about, Mr. Tiger?"

Sheena found humor in her description. "People really call him that?" she asked, always amazed at hearing that expression.

"Girl, the man is a force to be reckoned with in the courtroom."

Sheena smiled. "So I've heard."

"Well, I've seen him in action. If it weren't for Vincent Marshall, my cousin Chanel would have lost her children to her ex-husband. So … how did you meet him? Inquiring minds want to know!"

"I clerked for his partner, Bill Hart, my last year of law school."

"Oh, then you've known him for a while now?"

"Well, let's just say we've been acquainted for a while."

Carol moved to sit in one of the visitors' chairs in front of Sheena's desk. "I didn't know he was available. If I had, I would've hit on him myself!"

Sheena leaned her head back and bellowed with laughter. "And, what would your husband have to say about that?"

"Nothing! I wasn't married when I first met Marshall, and that means my whole life could have been different. Let me think about that for a moment … well, for starters, I probably wouldn't have married Glenn!"

Sheena shook her head. "Then, it's a good thing for Glenn you didn't know Marshall was single."

"Well, you better not let Jason find out you're going out with Marshall."

"Jason and I are just friends."

"Oh, so I guess Josephine was lying when she told me that you practically knocked him down when he walked into your office last Friday surprising you with his presence."

"I hadn't seen him in a long time. We're friends and I'd missed him. So yes, I was glad to see him."

Carol was silent for a minute, "Okay, you've told me that about a hundred times. I guess I need to believe it, especially now that he's moved to Atlanta and you're still here in Philly."

Sheena nodded. "Good idea."

Carol leaned forward in her chair, "You do know Josephine has a crush on you?"

"More office gossip, Carol?"

"This isn't gossip, it's the truth. You could see the jealousy on her face when she came out of your office after Jason arrived. I was standing right there at my desk minding my own business when I saw her walk past clearly upset. And me, being the concerned Christian person that I am, went into her office to make sure she was all right and see if there was anything I could do to comfort her."

Sheena shook her head, "You went fishing for information."

"Only to use it to help her."

"Hum uh."

"Well, anyway, she was clearly upset and I thought maybe you had said something to hurt her feelings. Now, you know I've noticed the strain on the working relationship ever since y'all stopped being bowling partners. So tell me... did she make a pass at you? Is that why you decided not to have her as your partner anymore?"

Everyone in the department knew Josephine Knight was a lesbian. That is, everyone except Sheena. She found out a few weeks after she'd asked her to take Jason's place in the bowling league becoming her new partner. One evening after practice, Josephine confirmed Sheena's newly forming suspicions. Sheena decided to end their bowling partnership because during her confession, Josephine assumed that Jason had asked for a transfer because he realized that Sheena was just like her, a lesbian. She further told Sheena that for that same reason she was uncomfortable around men. Then, to add insult to injury, Josephine finalized her comment with, *"they always find out about us, even if we deny it, what's in us comes out."* Sheena had felt so insulted that she walked away from her knowing that they could never truly be friends.

Josephine was half right. Sheena had indeed been struggling with her own sexuality but the thought of her being a lesbian was unthinkable. She didn't want anyone to know she'd ever even contemplated it.

Maybe her friend Miranda had been right. After Sheena complained to her about men looking at her as if she didn't have any clothes on, Miranda's reply was, *"men are gonna be mesmerized by your beauty even if you don't want them to be."*

Josephine didn't know her, so why had she listened to anything she had to say in the first place.

Sheena gave Carol a direct stare, "You know I'm not telling you anything. You know that don't you?"

"Yeah, well, you can't blame a girl for trying."

Sheena raised her eyebrows, "No, not at all."

"So, tell me, how did Marshall get you to say yes to a date with him? I mean, you've known him a long time – and you've never dated!"

"No, we've never dated, and for your information, this isn't a date! He helped a friend of mine out of a legal jam, and after everything was settled in mediation, he told me I owed him dinner and I agreed. That's all. So I feel a little obligated, especially since he didn't charge her one thin cent for his services."

Carol laughed. "Wow! He's not only smooth in the courtroom, but with the ladies as well! I'll tell you, girl, he sure did pull a move on you."

"Stop it," Sheena protested. "It's not even like that. It's only dinner. Besides, how many lunches have I purchased for you because I owed you one?" Sheena looked her co-worker straight in the eyes. "Yeah, you're remembering, I see you are. Believe me, I'm not interested in Marshall, and Marshall is not interested in me, not in that way," she said with finality. Sheena stood up, went to a file cabinet, pulled out a folder, scanned it, and pushed it back in place. When Sheena turned, Carol was looking at her suspiciously. Sheena hunched her shoulders responding to her glare, "What?"

"We'll just see, 'cause if he's as smooth as I think he is, it'll only take one dinner date for him to weave his charm all up and through here," Carol said as she fanned her arm in an up and down motion from Sheena's head to her toes.

"You are seriously tripping."

Carol's cell phone rang just as she began to laugh. "I'm not even going to answer it. I know that's my husband telling me he's downstairs waiting at the curb."

"Must be nice," Sheena remarked.

"Oh, don't give me that. Jason Jackson gave you curbside service all the time!"

Sheena half smiled, remembering how she and Jason had shared so many great times together ... and now they weren't speaking at all. "Well, don't keep him waiting. I'm going to finish up this file and get everything off my desk so I can have an easy Friday."

Carol stood and headed for the door. "Okay, I'm leaving. Everyone else is gone."

Sheena nodded. "I won't be too much longer."

"Is your car parked across the street?"

"No, I'm in the garage."

"Okay, then. You have a wonderful evening!"

"You do the same."

Sheena sat at her desk another twenty-five minutes before heading to the garage elevator. She checked her watch. "Quarter to seven" she whispered to herself. *I'll make it to the restaurant by seven-thirty,* she thought. *The Ben Franklin Bridge will be the best route to take.*

She spotted her car as soon as she stepped off the elevator. Taking her keys from her purse, she aimed the black remote to unlock her car. As she reached for the door handle, though, she was suddenly jerked backward.

"Jesus!" Sheena cried. Someone hit her in the face. She cried out again as she was knocked to the ground and was being kicked and punched at. Sheena tried instinctively to defend herself, but the garage started spinning around her and she stopped being able to fight back. Intuitively she balled herself into a fetal position and prayed.

She knew she was going to die.

Chapter Two

Sheena Daniels tried to open her eyes but she couldn't. She felt as if she were locked in her own body.

"Open your eyes, baby, please open your eyes." It was her mother's voice, and even though she couldn't see her, Sheena knew she was crying. *I'm not dead? No, I can't be. To be absent from the body is to be present with the Lord.* She knew she was still here on this bitter earth when she felt the soothing touch from her mother's hand to her face. She'd survived the attack.

"Open your eyes, baby," her mother pleaded again.

Sheena had never been a quitter, but was death so bad? Why was she still here, anyway? Her life was an absolute mess. She was struggling against her feelings of homosexuality, and to top things off, she'd lost the only man she'd ever loved. Jason Tyrone Jackson had been her only chance of having a normal life – and now he was gone and it hurt like hell.

"She's crying, look! She's in pain," she heard her mother say.

No, Mommy, I'm not in pain, she tried to say. But her mouth was not cooperating. Sheena tried to open her eyes, but she felt paralyzed. *Oh God, what is wrong with me? Why can't I move?* She struggled to move. Then, all of a sudden, her body completely relaxed and she drifted into a place of peace, in sleep.

Sheena heard a lot of voices as she slipped in and out of consciousness. Among the voices were those of her childhood friends, Ivy Jones Miller, Miranda Jones, and Jade Sanders-Parker. She heard them praying, both individually and collectively. The one voice she wanted to hear though was Jason's; but she never did.

It was time to take stock, since she clearly couldn't communicate. With her 32nd birthday approaching, Sheena felt she had accomplished very little in life – even though she possessed a Jurist Doctorate Degree from Rutgers University and was an attorney for the United States Department of Education. She was smart enough to pass the bar exam, but she wasn't smart enough to pass the game of life … or intelligent enough to keep her heart from being broken.

"The detective told me that Josephine didn't do this to her," she heard Jade say.

"She couldn't have, she was in Maryland when it happened," Sheena's mother answered.

"I still don't trust that woman. If I had my way, I wouldn't let her around Sheen."

"Jade, the woman is extremely upset about this whole thing. And now that we know for a fact that she couldn't have done this, we all need to treat her with the same respect we give all her other co-workers."

"What?" Jade was stunned. "She's gay, Ms. Christina, and she's the reason why Sheena's confused about her own sexual orientation."

"I have to trust that I have trained my child in the ways of the Lord, and I must be confident that she'll make good decisions for her life based on the morals I've instilled in her."

There was a long pause. "I guess you're right," Jade conceded.

There was some basis for Jade seeing Josephine as a threat. Ever since Josephine admitted being a lesbian, Sheena's begun questioning her own sexuality.

"I'm just concerned about her, Ms. Christina. I love Sheen like a sister."

"I know you do. You, Ivy, and Randi, you're like daughters to me. All of you have been friends since you were children and it's rare to hold onto such close friendships the way you all have."

"We are blessed," Jade agreed.

"Extremely," Christina nodded.

"It's just that I've seen a change in her since she's been hanging out with that woman. She even seems depressed sometimes."

"And you don't think that has anything to do with Jason?"

"Maybe..."

Sheena felt bizarrely like she was eavesdropping on their conversation about her. But their mention of Jason brought her thoughts to focus on him. The last thing he had said to her was, *"I need to let you go."* That's why he had moved to Atlanta in the first place, he wanted to move on with his life.

Just thinking about the conversation was more painful than the beating she'd just endured in the parking garage.

Beauty had afforded Sheena any man she wanted, though she never used her looks for personal gain. Being beautiful had actually been a burden on her; she'd always been defending herself against men who gawked at and flirted with her. As far back as she could remember, her mother had always said beauty would fade with time and in the end she would stand bare with nothing left except her personality. It was more important, she concluded, to be beautiful on the inside than on the outside. But as her teen years moved into womanhood, Sheena possessed curves that made her the envy of many women – and the fantasy of a lot of men.

The thing that bothered her most was that men never saw her for who she really was … well, that was the case until she met Jason Tyrone Jackson.

The last time she saw him had been less than a week ago. They had spent a whole weekend together, simply enjoying each other's company. It had been the best weekend she'd had in a long time.

But on Sunday evening, after they had attended Jade and Darrell's wedding, he told her he wouldn't be seeing her anymore. She remembered him saying, "I'm thirty-six years old. I want to get married. I want children. I don't want to live alone anymore, and I'm tired of rotating women in and out of my life." She felt crushed after he made that statement.

The situation was far from simple. Jason is Muslim and she is a Christian; and that was the main thing that kept them from being more than friends. In the beginning, she had no idea what the Islamic faith was about. So she attended the temple with him a few times. She researched the faith and found that it was totally different from Christianity … so converting wasn't an option for either of them.

That last weekend together had still been wonderful though. It had been months since they last saw each other. Jason had simply showed up at her office, and Sheena couldn't have been happier to see him. It had been as if Jason had never moved to Atlanta, as if they hadn't stopped seeing each other, and as if everything was as it should be: spectacular. But by the time Sheena

Reign 17

drove them to her apartment after attending Jade and Darrell's wedding, his whole mood had changed.

"You said you wanted to talk to me privately, so I thought coming back to my apartment was the best place for us to do that." He acknowledged her with a curt nod. Sheena had no idea what had happened between the wedding service and that moment. He had been silent throughout the whole trip back. She saw him catch the garter and then walk out of the church social hall. "You missed most of the reception. Where did you go?"

"I needed to think, so I caught a cab and went to my mother's house."

"Oh ... I'm surprised you came back," Sheena answered with a hint of sarcasm. Jason's mother never approved of her, simply because she wasn't Muslim.

Jason was somber. "Why are we in this predicament, Sheena? I've been thinking about it all weekend. When I caught that garter, I realized you and I would never marry, not since you insist we just remain friends."

Sheena walked into the kitchen. *So that's what changed his mood*, she thought. She returned with Jason's favorite flavored bottled water. Jason rejected the offer and sat on the chaise lounge.

Sheena's apartment wasn't an unfamiliar place to him, yet at that very moment, he was clearly feeling uncomfortable being there.

Sheena studied him for a moment. "I'm assuming the predicament you're referring to is your decision to move to Atlanta?"

He dropped his gaze to the floor. "That's not what I'm talking about, but I thought moving was best for us."

"Then what are you talking about, Jason?"

"I want more." He looked around the room. Spotting the photograph of Sheena and himself on the coffee table, he reached over and picked up the frame. "I'll never forget this day," he said. "I never had so much fun at an amusement park, even as a kid!"

"You're stalling. What's on your mind?" Sheena wanted to know.

Jason looked directly at her. "I love you," he confessed.

She braced herself, knowing now that this wonderful weekend had to have been the calm before the storm. With trepidation she answered, "And I love you."

"But it's not enough is it? Us ... just ... loving each other. I want more, more of you."

Sheena stood still, not uttering a single word. *Here it comes,* she thought.

"I was wrong for thinking we could remain friends, and that I would behave myself and be in control of my desire for you. I know now... after spending this weekend with you, I know it's impossible. We can't be *just friends.*"

She dropped her eyes, concentrating on the pattern of the carpeted floor.

"Us talking on the phone and being around each other like this makes things complicated. Even with so many miles between us, I can't do it and I can't move on while being so involved with you." He paused, waiting for Sheena to say something, but she remained silent, so Jason pressed on. "When I leave tomorrow, I won't be calling you anymore, and I don't want you to call me."

Sheena looked up at him abruptly. "But, you promised we'd always be friends!"

"When I told you that, I thought we would. But us being so close has damaged my chances of finding a wife and having a family. I need to let you go, Sheena."

Her eyes filled with tears. "You lied," she accused him. "You said we'd always be friends."

"Yeah, I did. And I was wrong. I'm sorry," Jason said, a tear sliding down his cheek.

She got a hold of herself. "That's why you moved to Atlanta anyway, right? You needed to get away from me, and here I am still pestering you. I'm the one who should be sorry." Sheena made a mental effort to be brave.

"There's nothing to forgive. I thought if we separated for a while, we'd realize just how much we cared for each other and realize that we were too in love to stay apart. I really thought that it would bring us closer together. But I was wrong. You're satisfied with just being friends, and I'm standing here right now wanting to pick you up, take you to your room, and make love to you until the two of us become one."

Sheena gasped putting her hand on her chest.

"You see, you find that appalling."

"No, I ... I don't."

"Then why did you react that way?"

"I was surprised... at your... choice of words... that's all."

There was a silence between them for a long moment. Jason finally spoke again.

"I'm thirty-six years old, Sheena. As I said, I want to get married, and I want children. And since I can't have that with you, we need to do what it says in one of your scriptures and I'll quote, Come out from among them, and be ye separated."

Sheena wanted to burst into tears. But she refused to allow him to see her cry, so she straightened her spine and said, "I understand. And, I'll comply with your wishes."

"No, you're not complying with my wishes; you're complying with the alternative which in my opinion is a very poor substitute."

"I'm complying with the choice that you're giving me. You haven't presented any other options."

"Yes, I did. I asked you to marry me."

"But I can't ... you know that. We don't even believe in the same God."

"Has that stopped us from being friends?"

"But marriage is different."

"Then convert."

"What!" She was appalled. He'd never asked her to do that before. Converting meant that she would no longer believe Jesus to be the Son of God.

"You heard me. Convert," he repeated, an edge of authority in his voice.

Sheena shook her head. "I believe that Jesus is a physical expression of an invisible God, one with Him, and I can't…"

"I already know how you feel. But don't tell me other options aren't available," he answered angrily.

"It's not like converting from Baptist to Methodist or even Catholic to Holiness," Sheena tried to reason with him.

"No, it's not." He leaned back and rested his arm on the back of the chaise lounge.

"We believe in two totally different doctrines!"

Jason smiled mirthlessly. "Yet, when we're together, our spirits soar as one." He rose and stood directly over her. "Why is that so?"

She hesitated to answer as she contemplated the question. Jason pulled her close to his chest and wrapped his arms around her. She really didn't want to fight with him. If he wasn't Muslim, she would have already been Mrs. Jason Tyrone Jackson. She loved him and there was no doubt about it. Then a scripture came to her mind, *for it's better to marry than to burn.* Maybe she should just marry him. That would stop both of them from being tortured. She rested her cheek against his solid chest and closed her eyes.

He kissed the top of her head and when he whispered again, "I love you," the scent of his cologne filled her senses ... and then the answer came to her.

"It's just emotions," Sheena said. "What we're experiencing isn't spiritual, but physical." She leaned back to get eye contact. "It's what our bodies crave. That's why you want to take me in my room and... and..." She couldn't even repeat what he had said he wanted to do to her.

"Make love to you until we become one?"

"Yes." She stepped out of his embrace.

"Look at me, Sheena. I love you."

"I know. And, God knows I love you. And I thought it may be better to marry than to burn."

"That's right. We're not hurting anybody but each other. We need to marry and move on so we can be happy."

"But for how long? We would be marrying for the wrong reasons. We'd be marrying because of our physical attraction – no, not even that, because of our hormones... Are we supposed to marry and do what we both know is morally improper and irresponsible because of our hormones?"

"I could live with it. You can serve your God. As a Muslim man, I can marry a Christian. So you see, you can continue to be a Christian and..."

"No! We are spiritual beings and we just can't ignore or separate our body from our soul. Marriage means we become one. How can we be one with you being Muslim and me being Christian?" She looked directly at him and, after taking a calming breath, she moved toward her front door. "You know what, you're right. We need to separate and leave each other alone. I promise not to call you or bother you ever again."

She wanted to be angry enough to not feel the pain of that decision. Not only did she feel pain, but depression immediately settled in. Tears that she was able to hold at bay fell freely because she couldn't control them anymore.

"We just put some medication in her IV," she heard an unfamiliar voice say.

"Thank you, nurse," she heard her mother answer. "As you can see, she's crying. She must still be in pain."

Chapter Three

Sheena was finally able to open her eyes. Even though the room was dim, she knew she was still in the hospital. She looked to her left and saw her mother sleeping on a cot.

"Mommy!" She tried calling, but it came out in a gurgle. There was, she noticed, a tube coming from her nose. Not only couldn't she talk, but her hands were bound. Sheena began to struggle to free herself, and then it began to feel as if she was choking.

"No, Sheena. You have to be still, baby." Her mother was at her side, touching her face while looking into her eyes.

Sheena wanted water. Her throat was dry and she tried to tell her mother. "Don't try to talk. I'm calling the nurse for you. I know you're in pain, baby." The truth of the matter was, she didn't feel any physical pain. She stared at her mother, wanting desperately to communicate.

A nurse walked in the room. "She's pulling on the tubes again?" The nurse asked.

"No, she's trying to talk."

Untie my hands. Sheena tried to say the words. But, all of a sudden she felt relaxed. And her mother began to moisten her lips with ointment. Sheena stared into her mother's eyes. "You're going to be all right, baby," she assured her. "You just need time to heal." She rubbed her hair. "You're going to be just fine. God has worked miracles on you."

Sheena tried to stay focused on her mother's face. But after a few blinks, she was asleep again.

Sheena was dreaming. She knew because she was standing near the ocean with the sand under her feet watching the tide roll in. It was a beautiful sight. She had never seen the horizon look so magnificent, nor had she ever felt such peace. She heard her name called and when she turned in the direction of the sound, there stood her grandfather. Instinctively she ran to him, her arms outstretched. "Poppy!" she cried with delight.

With a huge smile on his face and his arms opened wide, he greeted her. "Hey, my sugar dumpling!"

He was the only one who called her that. "I've missed you, Poppy." Taking the sight of him in, she realized her grandfather had passed away over five years ago. Stepping back, Sheena stared at his profile as he watched the sun melting on the horizon. Knowing she never felt such peace in all the days of her life, she figured this had to be heaven – especially since Poppy was standing next to her. That must mean she had moved on to the other side. "I'm dead," she announced.

Her grandfather turned to face her. "No, sugar, you haven't finished your job yet."

"What job, Poppy?"

He only smiled.

"Who did this to her?" Sheena turned toward the sound of the voices and saw no one. When she turned back, her grandfather was gone.

"Her face looks normal now." That was Jade's voice; but she didn't see her. She couldn't see anything through the dense fog.

"Thank God the swelling went down. Mother Evans said we would see a modern-day miracle, and she was right!"

Ivy. It was Ivy and Jade. But, where were they? She still couldn't see them.

"Pass me that Vaseline. Her lips stay so dry," Ivy complained.

Sheena felt her lips being moistened. "She's been in and out of consciousness for days now."

I was dreaming, Sheena thought. She had never had a dream that felt so real before. The dream was so vivid that she had to remember that she was in the hospital recovering from the attack. She wanted to open her eyes. *God, please let me open my eyes.*

"She's in God's hands."

Who was that? For a long time Sheena heard nothing.

Lying there, Sheena had time to think. She thought about a lot of things in her life and, coming to the conclusion that she was in deep trouble, she prayed. *Father, I know I'm not perfect. I have tried to live as you commanded. I've tried to be holy as you are holy. And I know that I've fallen short, not only in deeds, but in thoughts too. Please forgive me for every unclean idea. Sanctify my mind. I want to live pleasing in your sight. Forgive me for not spending more time with you. Forgive me for being disobedient and not...*

"Sheena, I know you hear me."

Prayer interrupted. *That's Jason,* she thought.

"I need you to wake up, just a moment, for me."

I hear you, Jason. Where are you?

She felt his hand on her own and felt him raise it. Then, she felt his soft lips touch her palm. She smiled. He then kissed her fingers and cupped her hand to his face. She realized there was no hair on Jason's face.

Jason always had a closely trimmed beard. When he began to pray, she knew it wasn't Jason. "I know you're going to restore her, Lord. You are a doctor that's never lost a patient."

Marshall? Sheena recognized his voice. She couldn't believe Vincent Marshall was here and was praying for her.

ಬಿಲ್ಲಿ

Sheena knew immediately that she had lost some time between Marshall's prayer and now, or was it Pastor Jones praying for her all the time and she just thought it was Marshall? "We know, Lord, that you are the author and finisher of our faith. We have fasted and prayed for our sister in Christ. Touch Sheena now from the top of her head to the soles of her feet."

Now she knew that there were a few people in the room as she heard them agree with the prayer being prayed.

"Regulate every single cell and make them function and line up as they are supposed to be. We are asking you today for an old-fashioned healing in this modern-day time. It's in Jesus' name we pray: Amen."

"Amen."

Amen.

"You need to go home, Christina. You need to get some rest."

"I'm not leaving her," Sheena's mother said between clinched teeth.

"Sitting here day and night won't change Sheena's condition."

"Why did God allow this to happen to her?" Christina asked.

Mommy's angry. Sheena could hear it in her voice.

"She's not suffering, Christina. However, *you* are. You need to go home and get some rest. I'm sure one of the girls will stay for a while."

"She's been in pain. I've been here to make sure they keep her comfortable."

"I'm sure they'll continue to do that while you're gone." Pastor Jones came closer to get a good look at her face. "Look at how God has mended her while she's been sleeping. When she first got here, I could hardly recognize her. God is truly amazing. She'll have to look at photos to see what trauma she's been through."

"I just can't imagine why anyone would want to hurt her. My God, Pastor, it had to be a robbery attempt or something. Anyone that knows her knows she'd give the blouse off her back to help anyone."

Mother Evans agreed with Sheena's mother. "She sure will. But knowing Sheena, she probably fought that bully. That's why they had to use their feet on her."

Pastor Jones nodded. "You're probably right, Mother."

"That doesn't answer my question. Why did God allow this to happen?"

"God does everything for a purpose, Christina," Mother Brown answered. "Some things ain't for us to know why. Even if we did, we might not understand it. God's thoughts are not our thoughts, and His ways are not our ways."

"He looks beyond the surface of emotions," Pastor Jones continued. "We've prayed to God. Now, let's trust and believe that He will answer and move according to our petition."

"Come on, Christina. Let us take you home. You're making yourself sick. Sheena is being taken care of, and now it's time to take care of you." Mother Evans rubbed her back in a comforting motion.

"I'm not leaving her. I'm not moving from this place." Christina was adamant.

"Well okay, if that's what you want to do. Suit yourself." Mother Evans patted her back one last time and moved to the exit. "I'll meet you in the car, Pastor."

"Okay, Mother. Have you eaten anything?" the Pastor asked Christina.

"Marshall brought me a plate about an hour ago."

"Marshall?"

"Yes, Vincent Marshall. He's a friend of Sheena's."

"Vincent Marshall. The name sounds familiar."

"He's the one that helped Jade with her legal matter a short while back."

"Oh, yes, I remember now. He and Bill practiced together."

"That's the one."

"Well, if you're sure you don't need anything. I'm leaving. I'm in prayer for you," Pastor said just before exiting the room.

Christina stood to run her hand through Sheena's hair. She put her lips to her daughter's ear. "I'll be right here waiting for you till you open your eyes, baby."

ଚ୦ଓଷ

Pastor Jones came into the lobby where his daughter sat with his niece and their friends. Ivy, Miranda and Jade all looked exhausted.

"I see you couldn't get her to leave, either," Ivy said to her father.

"No, she's firm. She doesn't want to leave Sheena alone."

"She's been here … what, a week now?" Miranda asked.

"Nine days," Pastor Jones corrected her.

"She's going to open her eyes by morning and she's going to stay awake," Miranda prophesied.

"I'm touching and agreeing on that in the name of Jesus," Jade proclaimed.

"Me too," Ivy agreed. "Has Ms. Christina talked to the doctor today?"

"Yes. He said the swelling in her brain is down and he feels strongly about a full recovery. So, at this point I think her body just needs time to heal."

"I think you're right, Uncle James. I'm going to the cafeteria and get me a sandwich. Then, I'm going upstairs to see about my mother."

"I was with your mother earlier. She fell asleep on me," Pastor Jones complained.

"She's on a lot of medication, Uncle James, you know that."

"I know, but sometimes she can't remember that I've been there. So, I started leaving her notes."

Miranda's mother had been fighting cancer for more than four years. For a while she really thought her mother had beaten the decease, but after a whole year of remission, it came back with vengeance.

Miranda smiled at her uncle. "She told me you do that."

"Well, I may be her brother-in-law, but I'm also her pastor. She needs to know I have a double concern for her."

"She knows, Uncle James."

"You girls have a good evening. I'm going to Cooper Medical Center to see Deacon Taylor."

Sheena's mother appeared in the doorway. "Ivy, Jade, come quick!" She turned dashing back down the hall.

Everyone rushed to follow her. When they entered the room, Sheena's eyes were open and she was struggling to communicate. They circled the bed.

Ivy leaned in close to her face. "Hey girl, you know we've been here waiting for you to wake up."

Sheena blinked several times.

"I told them you would be up by tomorrow," Miranda chimed in.

Sheena tried to talk again.

"You have a tube going down your throat and you're connected to some other things," Christina said to her daughter. "But the doctors all say you're going to be just fine." Sheena was still trying to talk and her mother placed her ear near her lips. A moment later she looked up. "She wants water."

Chapter Four

To Sheena, it felt like she'd been in the hospital only a few hours, but she knew it had to be much longer. She was unable to drink water, but she was allowed crushed ice and it felt so good in her mouth.

After an hour or so of being awake, Christina asked, "Do you remember what happened to you, baby?"

Sheena blinked her eyes twice. Then she made a writing motion with her right hand.

"Give her something to write with," Christina directed.

By the time they gave Sheena a pen and paper, the newscast on television had answered her first question: she had been in the hospital for over a week. She struggled to print her second question. *Who did this to me?* Her normally neat handwriting was unrecognizably sloppy.

Christina answered. "We don't know, baby. They're searching for the person. Your co-worker Josephine is helping with the investigation. I talked to her yesterday. They found two cameras that show the person coming in and out. But the camera was across the street, so they had to send the tape out so it can be enhanced."

Sheena, blinking her eyes, wrote, *I thought I was dead.*

"You gave us a fright for a moment there. We banded together and prayed, and God moved. You're going to be just fine."

How long will I have to be here?

"That, I don't know. But judging from the way you've healed already, it won't take long. The doctors all agree you are a miracle in progress. They thought in the beginning they would have to operate on you, but they didn't. Your healing has come from Heaven above."

Sheena wrote, *I heard you praying.*

"I told you she could hear us," Miranda said in triumph. The whole church has been praying for you."

Sheena blinked her eyes twice and began to write once again, *where's Jason?*

Christina looked at Ivy and she shook her head. Sheena's mother chose her words wisely. "I haven't seen or heard from him, and I don't believe he knows what's happened to you."

Disappointment edged across her face and was evident in her eyes.

"We haven't seen Jason, but Marshall's been here every day.

Sheena wrote, *I was supposed to meet Marshall.*

"I know. He's been praying for you, too. You have so many people that care about you. So don't worry about one thing, you hear me?"

Sheena blinked her eyes in agreement.

"Your father went to your apartment and he heard some disturbing messages on your answering machine. They were left the same day you were attacked. We shared it with the police and they recommended that we have your number changed. So we did, and we're in the process of getting your cell number changed too."

Sheena blinked her eyes again in understanding.

She cried every day for more than two weeks. A doctor diagnosed her mood as clinical depression. But her friends knew the real reason was Jason. She was grieving the loss of their friendship.

One month and three days after being rushed to Temple University Hospital in critical condition, Sheena was released. Recuperating at her parent's home, she only ventured outside to attend her follow-up medical appointments. She refused visitors other than her childhood friends; and her mood was dismal.

Something had to be done to get her out of the funk she was in. So Ivy and Marshall came up with a plan to get her out of the house and into a social atmosphere. She shared her plan with Bill – since she needed him to carry it out.

Bill asked, "So, she's already agreed to go to the lake with you?"

"With us," Marshall corrected.

Ivy shook her head. "Bill, I know I should've asked you before I made you a part of this scheme, but when I went to see her yesterday and she was just sitting in that room looking out the window and staring into space, I just..."

"No, Ivy, that's not what I meant. I'm just surprised she agreed to go. What did you say to her?" Bill asked.

"Well, I told a little white lie. Actually, part of it was Marshall's idea." She looked over at him and smiled.

"Okay, then, what is my role in this little white lie?"

"I went to her and said, 'I'm going to the lake,'" Ivy responded. "I told her that you and I wanted to spend some time together without the kids, and that we wanted to go to Marshall's parents' cabin."

Ivy remembered the conversation of the day before. Sheena had turned from the window to look at Ivy. "And, you need me to watch the children?"

"No, silly woman, I need you to go with me."

Sheena looked surprised. "Go with you?"

"Well, it's not like you have anything to do. You're still on the road to recovery and besides, I think it will be exactly what the doctor ordered: wonderful rest, peace and relaxation!"

"I have plenty of rest and relaxation right here." Sheena turned to look out the window again.

"Sheena, Randi can't go. She has to work, and Jade is working to get the school ready to open, as well as, studying for the state bar."

Sheena turned back to her. "So, I'm actually babysitting you."

"Yes, girl, I need a babysitter. I'm afraid I might jump that man's bones. Do you realize how long it's been since..." Her voice trailed off, realizing her friend had no earthly idea about such a thing. Sheena had never been married and, as far as Ivy knew, she was still a virgin.

"Three's a crowd, Ivy."

"No, Marshall will be there," she informed.

Sheena gave her an unreadable look. "Then, why can't he watch the two of you?"

Ivy put her hand on her hip, "Now what do you think people will say knowing I'm at the lake with two single men?"

"It doesn't matter what people think," Sheena shot back.

"Let's don't go there, okay. You know I can't do that. So, will you please go with me?

Sheena shook her head. "Ivy, I just want to stay home and…"

Ivy had to insist. "Sheena, please. You don't have anything to do for the next few weeks. It's only for a week."

Sheena's eyes widened, "a whole week? I haven't even fully recuperated from my injuries and you want me to go on a vacation with you?"

"Yes, and I've already asked your mother and she asked your doctor and both of them think it's a great idea. Seven days up in the mountains with fresh air and a change of scenery will do you good. We'll have a great time. I promise."

There was a long pause and Ivy gave her a pleading look. "Please," she added for effect.

"After that kind of look, I guess I have to go."

When Ivy finished telling her story, Bill asked. "So, all I have to do is pretend you and I are…"

"Sweet on each other," Ivy completed his sentence.

Marshall looked over at Bill, knowing that his friend surely didn't have a problem with that. Bill had been sweet on Ivy since the day he met her.

"Do you have a problem with this little white lie?"

"No," Bill answered. "I… I can do that…. No problem. No problem at all."

ಬಡಚ

Three days later; Ivy, Sheena, Bill, and Marshall stood outside the huge cabin by the lake. It had taken them six hours to drive there.

"Wow, this is beautiful, Marshall!" Ivy remarked.

"Well, thank you Ms. Ivy. My parents are the ones who actually own it. I'm just allowed to use it when they aren't."

"How long have they had it?"

"Since I was a kid, my grandparents owned it before that. It burned down about three years ago after being hit by lightning. The insurance company paid to have it replaced, and I was the one elected to ensure it was rebuilt."

All of them entered the living area. "Wow, Marshall. This is gorgeous! Isn't it, Sheena?"

"It sure is."

"How many bedrooms are there?" Ivy asked.

"Eight. All of them are the same. I did that so no one could complain about their amenities. The only thing that's different is the décor." He grinned. "Plus, each bedroom has a full bathroom with a Jacuzzi tub."

"Wow. Was it this nice before the fire?"

"No, it was old and in badly need of repair. Actually, the fire was a godsend."

"So what seemed to be evil turned out to be for your good?" Ivy elaborated.

"Exactly, my mother said a lot of family treasures were destroyed and she wishes she still had them, but she's learned to accept the lost." He smiled. "You and Sheena choose a room and get settled. Then we'll go out and get some groceries."

ಬಿಲ್

Later that evening, Marshall found Sheena sitting in a rocking chair on the back screened porch, enjoying the sounds of nature. "Hey."

Sheena looked up at him. "Hi."

"Mind some company?"

"Not at all, but I thought one of us was supposed to keep an eye on the lovebirds."

Marshall chuckled. "Well, they're out exploring the property, and I don't think they can get in any trouble doing that."

"You wouldn't like to put up a wager, would you?"

Marshall chuckled again. "No, I guess not. But, they are grown folks, you know."

"Yes, they are, but I'm my sister's keeper. She wanted me to look after her."

He paused for a moment. "Well, if they aren't back shortly, I'll go after them, how's that?"

"Fair enough," Sheena conceded.

Sheena had been quiet most of the trip and even more so since they arrived at the cabin, so just to make conversation Marshall asked, "When are you going back to work?"

"I'm not sure. I guess once my doctor releases me. That will dictate my return. But, I may take some extra time."

"I think taking extra time is a great idea."

Sheena gave him a little smile and Marshall couldn't help to think how beautiful she was and wondered who in the world would want to hurt her. Sheena may have recovered from her bodily injuries, but her spirit just wasn't the same. For a long while, Marshall studied her. He wanted to ask if she thought she and Jason would ever reconcile. He just didn't know how to bring it up without making it obvious he was interested in her.

Marshall had met Sheena just before she completed law school. At the time, she worked as a law clerk for Bill – who was his friend and partner. That had been more than five years ago, and Jason had always been on her heels. "I thought you and Jason would be married by now," he said without thinking. Sheena continued to look out into the darkness. He cleared his throat. "Sorry. I shouldn't have said that."

"It wasn't even part of our conversation. You caught me off-guard."

"Well, I was just wondering what has held the two of you back from doing what we all thought was obviously both of your destinies."

"Jason and I were friends, nothing more."

"You do realize he wanted more, don't you?"

Sheena turned to him with a blank look on her face. "How do you know that?"

"Because he told me, and I'm not the only one he told, either. Believe me, Sheena, when I tell you that he wanted much more than just a friendly relationship."

"Well, there is no more. There will never be anymore. We were friends and that's all."

"Were?"

She nodded, "were."

"The man is crazy in love with you."

"Jason doesn't love me. He doesn't know what love is."

"Do you know what love is?"

Sheena thought about the question a moment. "I was told that once you find love, you don't have to ask yourself if you are in love. You simply know it, feel it, and breathe it."

"But, I thought I saw all that in you."

"In me, yes. In him.., no."

Marshall looked at her and the strain he heard in her voice prompted him to ask, "He really hurt you didn't he?" Sheena said nothing. "What happened between you two?"

"Look, I really don't want to talk about Jason." She stood up and walked away before he could apologize.

He started to go after her, but Ivy and Bill appeared at that moment from the darkness. He turned to them instead. "I'm glad you're back, because I sure didn't want to come after you."

Both of them laughed. "You're really taking this chaperone thing seriously, aren't you?" Bill asked as he pulled the door open for Ivy to enter. He patted Marshall on the back just before he entered behind Ivy. Marshall trailed behind them both.

"Where's Sheena?" Ivy asked.

"She probably went to her room. I think I may have upset her."

"You argued?" Ivy asked accusingly.

"No." Marshall defended himself. "I asked her about Jason and she…"

"Why would you mention him, Marshall? Good grief!" Ivy stormed from the room, leaving the two men standing in the foyer as she went in search of Sheena.

Ivy tapped on Sheena's bedroom door. She could hear her whimpering from the other side. When she didn't answer, Ivy pushed the door open and went in. "What's wrong?" she asked as if she didn't know.

"I want to go home."

"Why? What did Marshall say to you?"

"Nothing."

"Don't sit there and tell me nothing when you're in tears. What did he do to you?"

"He didn't do anything. I just want to go home."

"Sheena, we just got here."

"I didn't want to come in the first place. You insisted I come."

"Yes, but you need to give this place a chance. It's beautiful here. Just try to enjoy it a little bit."

She paused a moment before asking, "Why didn't he come to see me, Ivy?"

Ivy didn't pretend she didn't know who she was talking about. "Sheena, sweetie, you have to let him go. You have to press forward and leave the past in the past."

"Tell that to my heart."

Ivy wrapped Sheena in her arms. "I know how you feel. I didn't want to love Ray after he hurt me so badly. I wanted to just turn the love off. But I couldn't. To this very day, I still love him. He's gone, resting in his grave, and I still love him." Ray was Ivy's deceased husband. They had been separated at the time he was killed in a car accident.

"Love hurts, Ivy. And, here you are in it again."

"Yeah, well, all love doesn't hurt. Ray and I had more good times than bad times and you know we did."

"How did he stop loving you, Ivy?"

"I don't believe he ever did. You see, once you love someone, I mean really love someone, you always love them."

"Then there's no hope for me. 'Cause I really do love Jason."

"I don't know, Sheena, if you really do love him."

"Why do you say that?"

"'Cause if you really did, him being a Muslim wouldn't matter to you."

Sheena made no comment as she thought about Ivy's statement.

"It's a good thing you never gave yourself to him. 'Cause if you had, you'd be more confused than you are now."

"I can't imagine being more confused than I am now."

"Oh, believe me, you could be. So what did Marshall say to you?"

"Nothing, he's just being Marshall," Sheena said as she wiped her eyes with the back of her hand.

Chapter Five

Ivy and Bill were in the kitchen preparing breakfast when Marshall came in. "Good morning!"

"Good morning to you, too. I just made some vanilla coffee," Ivy said.

"Smells good, I'd like a cup, please."

"Do you want me to fix you a plate?" Ivy asked him.

"Yes, but no eggs, please. Thanks." He pulled out a chair and sat down. "I owe Sheena an apology."

Ivy lifted her head from the toast to look at him. "Really, what did you do?"

"He didn't do anything," Sheena responded as she walked into the room. "Good morning."

"Morning," Bill and Ivy responded in unison.

"Good morning," Marshall responded flatly.

"I know you're hungry," Ivy said. "You didn't eat lunch or dinner yesterday."

"Yes, I'm starving," Sheena replied. Then she turned to Marshall. "And, you don't need to apologize to me. But, you *are* going to take me bowling."

Ivy giggled. "Oh, thank God, I don't have to go! I hate bowling."

"Marshall doesn't bowl," Bill informed her. "He's never bowled a day in his life."

Without hesitation, Marshall smiled at Sheena and said, "We're going bowling. I need to make a phone call first. When I'm done, we'll go find a bowling alley."

Sheena smiled in return. "Thank you, Marshall."

Ivy sat a huge plate of food in front of Sheena.

"You trying to fatten me up?"

"Eat what you can."

"I don't want pork bacon, Ms. Ivy."

"Like I'm going to forget you don't eat pork bacon, please. How long have I known you?"

"Most of my life."

"*All* your life, Ms Thing," Ivy replied in a huff. "That's turkey, for your information. I made pork for everyone else. I need you to…" Ivy stopped mid-sentence. "Forget it, you and I will talk later. Everyone is on their own for lunch. Bill is grilling steaks for dinner, so be here at seven p.m. sharp!"

Sheena and Marshall found the bowling lanes and played for more than two hours. Though Marshall had never had an interest for the sport, he found it enjoyable.

"You're really intense with this game," he said to Sheena after she beat him four games straight.

"I really like to bowl. For some reason, it relaxes me."

"Oh, I can tell you were loose. Talking smack to me, too."

"What? I was only encouraging you."

"Yeah, right," Marshall pretended to frown.

"Did I not help you and give you tips, but you said no - let me learn on my own?"

"That's because you can't be trusted. Putting me in that weird position and telling me to curb the ball when I release it."

Sheena tossed her head back and bellowed in laughter. "Get out of here man. I would never give you bad instructions just to win."

"Yeah, right," he answered, joining her in laughter.

Sheena began taking off her rented shoes, and her thoughts went to Jason. They had been bowling partners in a league for years. She thought she'd found a replacement for him when she started practicing with Josephine, but when that didn't work out, she'd given it up.

"Let me take your shoes back." Sheena looked up at Marshall and handed them to him. "Want something to drink?"

"No, I'm good."

"Be right back, then."

Sheena missed Jason. But, she decided she wouldn't cry anymore. She had to get control of herself and her emotions. Her love for Jason was what had been driving her emotions. She had to make decisions with her brain, and not with her emotions or heart. She still couldn't understand why he hadn't visited her in the hospital. Why he never called her. If the shoe had been on the other foot, sending flowers was the least she would have done. "God help me," she whispered in prayer.

She then thought about what Ivy had said to her. *I don't know, Sheena, if you really do love him. Cause if you did, him being a Muslim wouldn't have mattered.*

Marshall stopped her thoughts. "You ready to go?"

"Yes."

By the time they reached the car, Marshall could tell something was different. He turned the ignition to start the engine, and then turned to Sheena. "Your mood has changed. Did something happen while I was returning the shoes?"

Sheena turned her head to look out the side window. "No."

"It just seemed you and I were having fun and now you're in a dismal mood. Did I say something to…"

"No. You've done nothing. Let's find some ice cream."

"Ice cream?"

"Please…"

Marshall smiled and pulled out into traffic. The drive was silent and Marshall wondered what had changed her mood. Before he walked away, she was cheery and now – nothing. While driving through town he glanced over at her a few times; she continued to stare out the side window.

Marshall found an old-fashioned drive-in burger and ice cream place where the waiters skated to the car for service. After giving their orders, Sheena continued to stare out the side window.

"A penny for your thoughts," Marshall said.

Without looking at him, Sheena answered, "I was just wondering why I'm here."

"You're here because you asked me to bring you here."

"No, I mean why I'm here on earth. What my purpose is. Everyone has a purpose, and I've never found out what my purpose is."

"Your purpose could be for a single moment or it could be for a multitude of things."

"Do you know what your purpose is?" she asked him.

"My purpose is a multitude of things. I'm not here for one single moment in time. But to name that purpose, I'd say it's helping people through this crazy justice system. A few weeks ago, I helped a young father keep custody of his children. His children's grandparents were trying to take them from him."

"What was their reason for trying to take them in the first place?"

"Their complaint was simple. They thought they could be better parents for their deceased daughter's children."

"Goes to show you, you can sue anyone for anything."

"That's true, but they had a legitimate concern. You see, their daughter was a drug addict and so was my client for a while."

"Both parents on drugs, that's pretty bad."

"I agree. But my client got himself together and had been off drugs for about two years before this petition. For the last eighteen months, he's been working as a computer programmer, making about forty thousand a year. His girlfriend, on the other hand, could never kick the habit. But, he allowed her to stay in the home so he could try and help her. Well, she overdosed and died. And the parents wanted the children because of his history?"

"How did you win?"

"I really think it's because I asked the grandmother this simple question: What makes you think you'll be better for these children when you raised your own daughter and she turned out to become a drug addict and an unfit mother?"

"Wow, that had to have made an impact."

"When she looked at me stunned and her lawyer didn't object, the silence stretched and I had a feeling that one single question had won the judge over."

"You know they call you a tiger in the courtroom?"

"So I've heard, Marshall said as he watched her pick up her cell phone again. He assumed she was checking her messages. "You must be waiting on an important call."

Sheena turned to look at him. "Why do you say that?"

"Because you've checked your messages about five times since we've been out."

Sheena thought about his comment. He was right. Why was she checking her messages? Jason hadn't called by now and at this point; he had no reason to be calling her. Tears made her eyes glassy. She'd promised herself she wouldn't cry anymore and tears threatened to fall because she just realized Jason was out of her life. "Can I ask you something?"

"Sure, anything."

"Why did you come to see me every day while I was in the hospital?"

"Because I care about you and I wanted to be there for you and your family. Especially for your mother because she wouldn't leave your bedside for anything or anyone."

"But why would you want to do that, when we've never really been close?"

"I was the one you were going to meet when this happened. I was sitting in the restaurant fuming about how late you were when I got the call from Ivy that you had been rushed to the hospital."

"Really, you were upset?"

He laughed. "Yes, I was upset with you. Well, that was until I got the call. I left the restaurant and rushed to the hospital and, well, after that, I just kept coming."

"I heard you praying."

"Oh…"

"I thought you were Jason at first. But, I realized you were praying to God and not Allah. I remembered you saying something like you didn't get a chance for me to know you or something like that."

Marshall was astonished. "You heard me?"

"I heard a lot. Not just you, but a lot of other people too."

"That's remarkable."

"I thought about Jason a lot. I thought about our last time together and what he said to me. We didn't walk away on good terms. That's stuck with me and I wish I could get it out of my mind."

"You know, I've been afraid to fall in love, because I never wanted to risk getting hurt. But I've been told the best way to get over a heartbreak is to find love to heal it. When we have broken bones we stabilize it with a cast while the bone mends, right?"

"That's true, but if I put a cast on my heart I'm leaving it there," she joked.

"Don't make the same mistake I have."

"You put a cast on your heart?"

"Yes. I protected it so nothing would get in. But, let's get back to your question. My guess is that being created for only one moment in time is much harder than having multiple purposes."

Sheena shook her head. "You're probably right." She sighed. "I'm tired Marshall." He gave her his fullest attention. "I'm tired of pretending that everything is well with me, knowing deep in my heart it's not."

The waiter skated to the car with their orders. Marshall paid the bill and handed Sheena her dish of ice cream. Sheena took a spoonful and began to stare out the window again.

"You're not going silent on me again, are you?"

"I need to be silent. I've said too much already."

"I think you need someone like me to talk to." Sheena looked over at him. "I can be objective, because I'm not as close to you as Ivy or any of your other friends." He paused a moment. "I promise what you say to me will stay between us."

Sheena smiled at him. "I think I need a psychotherapist. Do you know a good one?" She was only half joking.

Marshall reached over and touched her shoulder. "I have a degree in psychology, so before you seek out a therapist and pay a ton of money, try me."

Sheena dropped her gaze. "Jesus is my therapist."

"Well, that's all well and good, but sometimes it's good to have flesh and blood as a sounding-board. Besides, I think you just need to talk out your feelings, and I'm a great listener."

"So are you saying I can tell you my deepest thoughts and you won't judge me or think I'm... I'm..."

"Crazy?" He completed her sentence.

"Yes," she nodded.

"I promise if you want to tell me things you haven't even shared with God, I will never convey it to a soul."

Instead of eating the ice cream, Sheena began playing with it and wondering if she could really share her most intimate thoughts with Marshall. Without warning she blurted out, "I wanted to die." She waited for him to react and when he didn't even flinch, she continued. "I couldn't understand why the Lord didn't just take me home." Sheena put the top back on the ice cream and continued. "When I was being kicked and beaten I remember thinking, I'm going to die, and I wanted to die. Why should I keep living? I wasn't living that abundant life and for the last few years I've been miserable and just holding on to my faith. I'm in love with a man that doesn't share my beliefs and..." Sheena let out a sigh, and then looked over at Marshall who was staring at her. "You promise this remains between us, right?"

Marshall nodded, "you have my word."

"I figured that I was being punished for having impure thoughts. You see, I know what the Bible says, and I know that I must adhere to all the rules. I know I'm under the law of God. And yet I've allowed things to enter into my mind that are wicked."

"What kind of things?"

"I don't know how to tell you this other than to just say it." She hesitated for a moment. "For a while..." She paused again as if she'd changed her mind about telling him.

"It's okay. Just say it," he encouraged her.

"There's a woman that I work with and she seems to think that I'm confused about my sexuality."

"Why does she think that?"

"I don't know. She said what's in me will come out."

"So — are you confused?"

She hesitated a moment. "Yes."

That revelation threw Marshall for a loop, but he never showed an outward sign.

"Jason is the only man I've ever felt comfortable enough with to date. So I really wanted things to work between us. I even thought about marrying him."

Marshall took Sheena's hand and kissed it. Sheena was surprised by the gesture. "So Jason was your first heterosexual relationship?"

Sheena gave a weak smile. "No. I've dated other guys before, but never for any length of time. Jason and I had something special. Being with him was like hanging out with Ivy, Randi, or Jade."

"Oh, I see."

"We talked about everything."

"Everything?"

"Everything," she confirmed.

"So you talked to him about these feelings as well?"

"Yes. He ignored them saying that I feel that way because guys are always gawking at me, which has forced me to not trust men in general."

Marshall nodded his understanding and Sheena wiped at a tear that threatened to fall. "How long have you felt this way?" Marshall asked.

"I don't know. I guess it's only been lately. It's not like I've thought this all my life. To tell the truth, the thought of me being a lesbian scares the hell out of me, and I find it repulsive. God knows I don't want to be that way."

"Well, some things are simply out of our control."

"Then I'm praying for total control. I want a husband, Marshall. I want two point five children and the house with the white picket fence."

He smiled. "I hear you."

She gave him a weak smile in return. "I just want to be normal." She sighed. "Can you image me in a lesbian relationship?"

"No, I truly can't. But some of the nicest people I know are gay and you'd be just another nice person who is gay."

Sheena sucked her teeth. "I wouldn't act on it, no matter what."

Marshall studied Sheena's profile and wondered how a woman of her distinguishing traits could ever think she was anything other than what God had made her. Nefertiti had nothing on this woman. "You know, Sheena. I'm a firm believer that you must be true to yourself."

"How can one be true to himself if they're confused?" she asked.

"You have to get to the root and find out how what you are thinking came to be."

Reign

"Get to the root... I just told you I'm confused, and I'm presumed to know how to get to the root? Please," she said and sighed.

"Well, if you're confused, how do you know you're truly gay? I mean... is it that you've never enjoyed sex with men?"

"Marshall, I've never had sex with anyone. Well, let me rephrase that. I've only been with one man intimately and that wasn't a full experience."

"So what you're saying is you're still a virgin?"

Sheena turned her head to look out the window. "I'm almost thirty-two years old. Have you ever heard of such a thing?" Her tone was agitated.

Marshall took both her hands and changed the direction of the conversation. "I had a wife."

She turned to him. "Really? I didn't know you had been married!"

"Yeah, I was. Right out of undergraduate school. I was working a full-time job and going to law school." He shifted position. "Anyway, she came home one day and told me she had a prescription filled for me and that I needed to take it. I knew I'd been coming home tired and not paying her a lot of attention so I just figured it was vitamins or something."

"But it wasn't?"

"No. It was an antibiotic for Chlamydia."

She thought for a moment. "That's a venereal disease, isn't it?"

"Yeah, one of the silent ones, I didn't even know I was infected."

"How did she find out she had it?"

"She went to the doctor for her regular six-month check-up to refill her birth control prescription. Like me, she had no symptoms, but a routine test revealed that she was infected. When I first questioned her about it, she told me it was nothing and to just take the medication. But the next morning, I called the doctor whose name was on the bottle and he asked me if I'd been with anyone other than my wife. I was honest with him and told him no, and that's when he told me that if I hadn't been with anyone other than my wife, then my wife got it from someone and gave it to me. He told me that it could only be contracted through sexual contact."

"You must have been devastated, hearing that!"

He nodded ruefully. "Oh, I was more than devastated. I had a whole range of emotions hit me all at once. I left work and went home to confront her. She tried to tell me I was the one that gave it to her, when I knew that I'd been faithful. We argued for hours before she admitted her infidelity, and then I found out that I'd never satisfied her. So she made it my fault that she cheated on me. Anyway, we separated." He looked out the window for a long moment before turning back to face her. "Not long after that, I found out she was terminally ill. I brought her back home and she passed away from a respiratory disease two months after I graduated from law school."

Sheena reached out and squeezed his hand. "You're a good man, Marshall."

"My family said I was a fool," he said sadly and smiled. "After she did that to me, I said that I would never trust another woman. I never allowed another woman to get close enough to hurt me again. As you can see, I certainly never married again. That's why I'm forty-one years old with no children, no wife, no home, and no love of my own."

"Maybe you and I should get together," she said jokingly. "It would be a business deal. Since you don't trust women and I don't trust men, we'd make a perfect match."

"You're probably right. We could draw up an agreement. Make it real business-like."

"Yes, we could. We could say how many children we'd have."

"Two point five, no doubt," Marshall joked along with her.

"Exactly, and we could take two vacations a year."

"Absolutely, one with the children and one without, and it would have to be a place both of us could enjoy," Marshall added.

"That sounds good. And while we're at it, we might as well include in our contract where we're going to live," Sheena continued.

"Well, since we're having children, we may as well live in the suburbs, because we can't raise our children in the heart of the city or in a high-rise apartment."

"You have a point." Both of them laughed. Then Sheena turned serious. "Think there's any hope of us finding spouses?"

"My hope is built on God's promise to me that I could have a more abundant life."

Sheena smiled. "Let's get back and check on Ivy and Bill. You know we're supposed to be babysitting them."

Chapter Six

Miranda had just received the news she'd been dreading for three years. The cancer her mother had been fighting had finally reached her bladder and lymph nodes. Death was imminent.

Miranda sat stunned, after hanging up the phone. How was she going to tell her mother? How were they both going to deal with this?

"Randi." She looked up and saw her mother standing next to her. "What's wrong?"

No sense in putting it off. "That was your doctor," she answered with regret, tears flooding her eyes.

"Oh," was said the only response.

Miranda took a deep breath to steady herself. "He called to…"

"I already know," her mother interrupted her. Miranda looked at her. "What do you mean, you already know?"

The older woman smiled. "I've known for a while now. I'm going to be with the Lord. I've been trying to prepare you."

Miranda stood there, not believing her ears. "Mama, why didn't you tell me?"

There was gentleness in her voice. "I've been a burden on you too long, Miranda. You can't even date because of me."

"That's not true."

"Then why do you only go to church and work?"

"I go out," Miranda protested, allowing herself to be sidetracked so she didn't have to talk about the only really important thing between them. "I'm out with Ivy and them once a week and I…"

"Hang out right here unless I'm in the hospital."

"Mama…"

"That young man you went to Jade's wedding with keeps calling here. Why won't you return his calls?"

She shrugged. "I'm not his type."

Her mother smiled. "Too late, he called here earlier today, and I invited him to dinner."

"Why did you do that? I don't want to see him," Miranda protested.

"I did it because he told me he needed to talk to you and you wouldn't return his calls."

"Mama, I really don't want to see him. He's a liar straight from hell."

Her mother took her hand and led her over to the kitchen table, where they both sat down. "Now, you tell me. What lie did he tell you to have you so tied in knots?"

Miranda sniffed. "Last week I found out he owns the company I work for. He's my boss's boss."

"And he'd told you he wasn't?" her mother asked.

"He didn't tell me anything. I found out by reading an article in the Tribune."

Her mother smiled. "Then, he never lied. He just neglected to tell you."

"That's the same as lying. Besides, he's only calling because I put in my resignation."

"Randi…" Her mother's voice was laced with surprise.

"I have another job. I'm not stupid enough to close a door before I have another to go through. My mama didn't raise a fool." She smiled, and her mother returned it.

"That's probably why he didn't tell you in the first place. He knew how you would react, which to me is just plain silly. So, what if the man has a business that's thriving? Just be grateful he has a mind to be a head and not a tail."

Miranda could feel the tears pressing against the backs of her eyes. "Right now I'm not concerned about him or myself. I'm concerned about you."

Her mother made a gesture of dismissal. "Don't you worry 'bout me. I've lived my life. My tour is over and I'm not mad about it, and I ain't afraid of dying. Dying is a part of life."

"But Mama, you're still young, you...."

She reached out and took Miranda's hand. "I'm tired, baby. I don't want to fight anymore. The only reason I put up a fight this long in the first place is 'cause of you. Losing both parents so soon together just didn't seem fair, so I asked God to extend my time and he answered my prayer. I got three extra years and without a lot of pain, thank you, Jesus. So, I don't want you to worry 'bout me. I'm going home to be with the Lord and I'm ready to see your daddy, my mama, and my own daddy. My heart is fixed and my house is in order. So, don't you worry 'bout me. I'm just askin' God to not let my suffering be too long."

The tears were flowing now. "Mama," Miranda sobbed.

"Come here, baby." She moved her chair closer to her mother's and her mother wrapped her arms around her. "Everything is gonna be just fine. I came in this world alone and I'm leavin' the same way I came." She rubbed her daughter's back. "Don't you fret none. I'm leaving you, but God will never leave you nor forsake you."

Miranda hiccupped on the tears. "You're so much more stronger than me, Mama."

"You come from me and your daddy and he was much stronger than me. You're much stronger than you think. You just hold on to God and never let go."

Miranda nodded and rubbed her eyes in an effort to compose herself.

"Now, that young man is coming to dinner tomorrow. What do you want to have?"

ಬಿಂಗ

When Sheena and Marshall returned from the bowling ally, they found the house empty. Sheena went straight to her room to rest.

Resting was the last thing on Marshall's mind. He couldn't stop thinking about what Sheena had shared with him. He pulled out his notebook computer and began to surf the net, looking for information about depression. He was sure that was part of her problem. After researching the subject, he placed a call to a therapist friend named Mary Taylor. Remembering he'd promised not to tell a soul about their conversation, he asked Mary general questions about depression. Then he repeated the entire conversation he and Sheena had without identifying who she was.

"Oh, so this confusion about her sexual orientation is just developing?" Mary asked.

"I guess so. What I can't understand is why would something like that develop after all these years?"

She sighed and asked, "I hope you're not asking me for a diagnosis with so little information?"

"No, I was wondering if you could point me in the right direction so I could do a little research on my own, that's all."

"Okay, then. Your friend's situation sounds similar to a case I had some years ago. Actually, he and I are very good friends. We grew up together and he was raised a devout Christian. He dated and fell in love with a woman who I thought was not good for him. But he married her anyway. About three years into the marriage, he came to me saying the same thing you said your friend is saying. He said he never knew he was gay until recently. But what he didn't tell me was that he caught his wife with another man. At the time, I didn't understand that he was hurt and was sinking into depression. He and his wife separated. In the very beginning he told me exactly what your friend told you, he had not acted on his newly found sexual feelings. He said he was afraid and that he didn't want to be gay, so he asked me to recommend a therapist. After a few sessions, he told me that he was suffering from a form of OCD, and that he wasn't gay at all.

"OCD?"

"Yes, it's called HOCD - Homosexual Obsessive-Compulsive Disorder."

"I've never heard of that."

"I wouldn't expect you to. But, there's a real difference between Homosexual Obsessive-Compulsive Disorder and actually being homosexual."

"How do you tell if someone is suffering from this Obsessive Compulsive Disorder or if they're really gay?"

"Well, you just told me that your friend told you they just recently developed these feelings, right?"

"Yes."

"Well, OCD is a type of anxiety that happens when there is a problem with the way the brain deals with normal worrying, troubles, or doubts."

"But I've heard of OCD, and it's like cleaning compulsively."

"That's one way it manifests. But in my experience, having intrusive thoughts about being a homosexual and doubting your own sexuality are symptoms that characterize a subtype of Obsessive-Compulsive Disorder, sometimes called Homosexual OCD or HOCD. Get on the net and do a little research. But now, I don't want you to think that I'm telling you that your friend is suffering from that."

"I know. I just wanted to get some direction on how to help her." He hadn't meant to say that.

"So, it's a woman?"

"Yes, and please keep this between us. I promised her I wouldn't breathe a word to anyone."

"Don't worry," she assured him. "I still don't know who it is, unless you want to tell me."

"When pigs fly," Marshall joked.

"Okay, well, good luck."

"Mary?" He tightened his hand on the receiver.

"Yes?"

"I know you're not taking any more patients because you're trying to retire, but if she decides to get help, would you consider accepting her? With you I'd know she's in good hands."

There was a pause before she answered. "I'd do it for you, Vincent. I can tell she means a lot to you."

"Thanks, Mary."

After reading more information, Marshall felt somewhat relieved. He hated to think that Sheena suffered from HOCD, but for him, it was better than her being a lesbian or bisexual.

"Hey, whatcha doin'?" Ivy asked, startling him.

"I was just researching some information," he answered as he closed the window of the site he was reading.

"Hum. Dinner will be ready in an hour," she responded.

"Oh, okay. You need help with anything?"

She laughed. "Oh, like you can help me."

"Ivy, I can do lots of things," he protested.

She grinned. "Really? Like what?"

"I can mix the salad, heat the bread…. I can even make lemonade… or…

"I get it. No, I don't need any help," Ivy chuckled.

Bill came into the room. "Hey, did you and Sheena find a bowling ally?"

"We sure did," Marshall answered. "Not too far away."

"Good, did you enjoy it?"

"She kicked my butt and I vowed to practice and give her a run for her money in the coming months."

"I'm sure you will too," Bill snickered. "I'm grilling steaks. You like yours well done, right?"

"Absolutely! I don't want to see any blood in my meat."

"Okay, I'm going back to the grill."

Ivy looked at Marshall suspiciously.

"What?" he asked

"Nothing, I'm leaving so you can finish what you were doing."

He nodded and turned back to his computer. As Ivy was leaving the room, she almost collided with Sheena. "Where were you?"

"I took a nap," Sheena said. "I was tired from whipping on Marshall."

"Ha," he said, not looking up from the computer. "Give me a little more practice, and we'll see if you'll still be talking smack a few months from now!"

Sheena and Ivy laughed, and Ivy slipped out the door. Sheena turned to leave too when Marshall called out, "Hang on a minute, Sheena, I found some information on the net I want you to read."

He shared the HOCD site information with her. At first Sheena read the lines he indicated while she was standing, but then moved to a chair next to him to read the information more thoroughly. "Wow, I've never even heard of this!"

"Well, I'm not a doctor, but it may be something for you to think about."

"Well, it sure looks like I need to contact a doctor."

"It's probably a good idea."

"They mentioned medications like Prozac, Luvox, and Zoloft. I certainly haven't heard anything good about those medicines," Sheena commented.

"Well, you don't even know if you have this particular problem until you get a professional diagnosis."

"There's no coming back from this. There's no cure," Sheena noted.

"There's no cure for homosexuality either."

Sheena smiled. "True. And for sure, I'd rather be HOCD than a lesbian. Maybe I can deal with this on my own without professional help."

Marshall disagreed. "I wouldn't advise it."

"I don't know anyone that I could see."

He cleared his throat. "I do. I have a friend named Mary Taylor. She's semi-retired and hasn't been taking any new clients, but she's a good friend of mine and I trust her."

"She's a good friend of yours?

"A very good friend."

"If she'll see me, this still remains between you and me?"

"Yes, I promise and I won't tell a soul."

Impulsively, she gave Marshall a tight hug. He was tingling from it all evening.

Chapter Seven

Miranda's mother had set a beautiful dining room table using her best china and flatware. The last time Miranda could remember her mother dressing such a beautiful table was for her father's birthday dinner, more than five years ago. Kyle had brought a bottle of white wine, not knowing that her mother never served alcohol. Miranda was surprised when her mother took the bottle with a simple word of thanks, but she did let him know she would be serving something different for dinner. Miranda was stunned. When she looked at her mother, she simply shook her head.

Miranda's mother had prepared dinner as if serving royalty. She served a fresh garden salad, prime rib, mixed vegetables, baked potatoes, and her famous homemade carrot cake.

"Everything looks lovely, Mrs. Jones."

"Thank you, Kyle. I hope it tastes as good as it looks. I haven't had the energy to cook in a long time."

"I'm sure it will."

Miranda's mother looked at her daughter. "Will you say grace, please?"

Miranda turned to Kyle. "I think Kyle should do the honors."

Without hesitation, he answered, "Okay, let's bow our heads. Father, we'd first like to thank you for this fellowship. We ask that you bless the food and bless the hands that prepared it. Let this food be nourishment to our bodies, in the name of Christ Jesus we pray, Amen."

Miranda's mother smiled. "Thank you, Kyle."

He nodded. For most of the meal, they ate in silence. Kyle praised Mrs. Jones' cooking and truly liked everything that was served. The quiet meal was exactly how Miranda wanted it. The less said the better. She was counting the minutes until this whole ordeal was over. She still couldn't believe her mother had invited this man to their home in the first place.

The silence was over when her mother asked, "So, how did you and Miranda meet, Kyle?"

"Her car broke down and I stopped, offering my help."

She smiled. "How long ago was that?"

"I don't know. I guess it was about three months ago, wouldn't you say, Randi?"

"Something like that."

Kyle laid his fork down. "I'm sorry, but there's no good time to say this. Miranda's been upset with me ever since we attended her friend's wedding, and for the life of me I don't know why." Kyle turned to Miranda and continued. "If I said anything to offend you, I'd like to know what it was so I can apologize."

She sniffed. "It's nothing you said, but since you brought it up, it's something you did."

"What did I do?"

"You stared at a woman who accompanied a friend of my friend's husband. You did it disrespectfully and it bothered me."

Kyle looked at her as if he didn't know what she was talking about.

"Oh, don't play dumb. You know who I'm talking about. 'Ms. One Hundred And Five Pounds', soaking wet, who just happened to be your ex-girlfriend."

Reign

"Oh, you're talking about Nicole?"

"Exactly, you ignorant snake."

"Miranda," her mother warned.

"No, Mama, he needs to know that I didn't appreciate him gawking at her all afternoon. My feelings were hurt," Miranda said.

"Oh, I see now. I understand how you could have been misled."

"Misled? There was nothing misleading about the whole thing. As a matter of fact, she approached me and told me that the two of you were ex-lovers. Those were her words, not mine."

"Miranda, let me explain," Kyle pleaded.

"You don't need to explain anything. I understand perfectly. You gawked at that woman from the moment you laid eyes on her. You never gave me a moment of the attention you gave her."

"Randi...," he tried to speak.

"As a matter of fact, I want you to leave," she announced with hostility.

"Miranda... let the man have his say," her mother intervened.

"I really don't want to hear any excuses from him, Mama."

Kyle sat there with his head bowed. "Then, I'll tell your mother my side of the story."

"That's fine. Then, I'm leaving." Miranda stood up.

"Miranda, sit down!"

Miranda stood her position. "Mama, I don't want to hear..."

"I said sit down this instant," her mother said with authority.

She immediately slid back down onto her seat.

"If you ain't just like your daddy." She looked over at Kyle. "She can be hot-headed sometimes. Go on. Tell your side of the story, Son."

He looked directly at Miranda. "It's true. Nicole and I dated for six years - two years of high school and four years of college. At the time, she wasn't a hundred and five pounds soaking wet. She was more like one hundred and ninety pounds soaking wet."

Miranda looked surprised.

"She had gastric bypass surgery, because she wanted to be thin. She wanted to be attractive to more men than just me. After the operation, she began to lose weight quickly. But, that wasn't the only thing she lost. As she shed the pounds, her personality went with it. I lost her to vanity. She became someone I didn't like. The sweet and loving person that I knew had vanished. She became wild, and I just couldn't deal with it. And, if you don't believe me, ask my grandmother, she'll tell you." He paused. "My guess is she never mentioned that she weighed nearly two hundred pounds at one time."

"She never mentioned anything like it."

Miranda's mother said, slowly, "But she told you they were once lovers. She didn't say that they dated, but were lovers. That means she wanted you to react the way you did, and you fell for it."

"No, she just said that you broke up after she showed an interest in something other than you."

Kyle smiled. "Well, I'm telling you the truth. You're right, I did stare at her, but not because I was attracted to her. It was because I couldn't believe how unhealthy she looked. The last time I saw her, she weighed about a hundred and fifty pounds or so. To me she looked sick and I was stunned. But, I promise you it had nothing to do with you at all. And, I do apologize for making you feel uncomfortable, and I'm asking you now to please forgive me."

"All is forgiven. But, why didn't you just tell me?"

"I didn't know that's what you were upset about. Why didn't you just tell me what you were upset about?"

"I was hurt and I didn't feel as if you owed me an explanation for your actions, so I just summed it up as another date disaster."

"But if you had asked me, I would have explained everything to you and then we wouldn't have lost these last few months when we could have been getting to know each other." Kyle turned to Miranda's mother. "Thank you for inviting me, Mrs. Jones, because if you hadn't, I probably would have never found out why your daughter avoided me like poison."

"I'm glad the both of you were able to straighten this out. Now that you know it was all a misunderstanding, maybe you can pick up your relationship where it left off," Mrs. Jones answered.

"That would be nice," Kyle agreed.

"I think you all need more time to talk, so I'm going to my room so you two can have a little privacy."

"Mama, we don't need privacy."

"I think you do. Kyle, she's stubborn just like her daddy, but being stubborn was one of his greatest characteristics."

"I'll keep that in mind."

Her mother smiled, picked up her glass of water, and exited the room.

Miranda shook her head and then turned back looking at the mess she knew she had to clean up. "I need to do the dishes."

"Leave the dishes and go into the living room," her mother yelled from the next room. "And, that's an order!"

"Come on," Kyle beckoned, leading her to the living room. "I really like your mother."

"Yeah, she's pretty cool."

After a moment Kyle asked, "So, you thought I was looking at Nicole because she's thin?"

"Well, I figured that was one of the reasons. Then when I found out she was your ex, I figured you still carried a torch for her."

"You couldn't have been more wrong. Believe me when I say I admire all types of women and I've dated women of all shapes and sizes, but for some reason, I'm attracted to thick women. I don't know why, I just am. When we met, I knew you were different from any other woman I'd ever met. You stayed in the car until you felt safe. You remember that?"

"I was taught to do that. There are a lot of crazy people in this world."

Kyle nodded his understanding. "When we talked in the restaurant that day, I knew I wanted to get to know you better. Your conversation was intelligent, and I enjoyed your company. You remember when I took you to meet my grandmother?"

Miranda nodded.

"She said to me, I like this one, Kyle; she's a woman after God's own heart."

"I really like your grandmother, too." She paused. "Kyle, why didn't you tell me you owned the company I worked for? I really would like to know."

"First of all, it isn't my company. My parents own the company. I work for them. And, I didn't tell you because I wanted you to get to know me first."

"Well, you do know that I would never mix business with pleasure?"

"So does that mean you don't want to date me?"

Miranda fidgeted. "I like you, Kyle. That's probably why I was so hurt when I thought you were interested in another woman. But I think it will be best if we just remain friends."

"I had a feeling you were going to say that." He sighed and looked away, discouraged.

Miranda bit her lip and thought about what to say. She really didn't want to hurt him. "So much has happened between us. I think since you've seen the stubborn side of me, that it's best we be friends. Besides, I've gotten over you and I think I'd just like to leave it that way."

He looked back at her. "Does this mean you'll take back your resignation?"

She shook her head. "No, it's time for me to move on."

"So you're going to work for the City of Camden?"

"Yes. I'll be working with their CDBG and Home Funding Programs."

"You know, Chris is really upset with me. He said you were the best draft person he had in years."

"I'll miss Chris, too."

ଆଓ

Ivy, Bill, Sheena, and Marshall all sat in the hot tub on the back porch that was made to hold six people. "I talked to Miranda this evening," Ivy said.

"Oh, that's right," Sheena chimed in. "Her mother invited Kyle over for dinner. How did that go?"

"She said it was rough at first, but then she found out that the whole thing that happened at Jade's wedding was a misunderstanding." Ivy gave them the full details. "She said he apologized and she accepted it, and now it's all behind them."

"That's what I'm talking about. You women are always assuming something," Bill commented.

"Well, if you ask me, I think she had a legitimate reason to think what she did," Marshall added.

"Yes," Sheena agreed.

"Well, I'm just glad he really wasn't as cruel as I thought he was. I have a new respect for the man," Ivy confessed.

"Since things are straight now, maybe she doesn't have to leave the job she loves so much," Bill said, sliding down in the tub to feel the hot water bubbling around his neck.

"No, she's still leaving. Her last day is Friday. Once she gets through these last five days, maybe she and Kyle can find a way back to each other. Randi really did like the guy," Ivy declared.

"That's all good news." Bill straightened up again. "On another topic, I forgot to tell you all that I've decided to represent Pastor Owens in his divorce."

"What?" Ivy almost yelled. "Bill, why?"

"The man deserves a good attorney, so I'm going to help him."

Ivy shook her head. "Well, I hope his wife sticks it to him. Miranda was always right about that man."

Sheena laughed. "She sure was. She knew he was a two-timing whore before the evidence came out."

"Well, just because the man is in love with another woman doesn't mean he shouldn't have a good lawyer," Marshall said. "That's the point of the system."

"Well, both of you knew Ray was unfaithful to me, and neither of you would represent me in a divorce," Ivy reminded them, pouting.

"Now, Ivy, you know that was different. I was Ray's attorney and that was clearly a conflict of interest. I could have been disbarred," Bill responded.

"You've been in love with Ivy since you laid eyes on her. You should have been disbarred for that," Marshall retorted, knowing Ivy had no idea he was totally serious.

Bill paused, not believing that Marshall had been so honest. He looked at Ivy. "I stand accused and guilty of the charge," Bill confessed. "But, I never disrespected Ivy or Ray. I stayed my distance. As a matter of fact, I have never dated a married woman."

Sheena knew how Bill felt about Ivy. Sheena had confronted him about it the day of the funeral when she saw how protective he was of her. At that time he tried to deny it, but the truth was in his eyes.

"None you know of," Marshall retorted.

All of them laughed.

Marshall leaned back and rested his head on the headrest. "Sheena and I are getting married."

Sheena slowly turned her head to look at him.

"We decided that since we believe in doing things business-like, we're going to put together an agreement of marriage for ourselves."

Sheena smiled. "That's probably the only way I'll marry anyone."

"An agreement, huh?" Ivy replied, going along with the joke. "That might not be a bad idea. Bill, maybe we should put a marriage contract together listing everything we expect from each other."

"I don't need a contract. My love for you is all I need. That is the contract."

"Oh, how sweet," Sheena said and sighed. "One of these days maybe, just maybe I'll have someone to love me that much and in that way." Sheena rested her head on the hot tub cushion, closing her eyes.

Bill looked at Marshall and mouthed to him as Ivy looked on, "You better tell her how you feel."

But, Marshall knew this wasn't the right place or the right time.

Chapter Eight

Miranda walked into the KBW Engineering Firm at 8:15 sharp. She'd been working for this company for almost five years. As usual, she greeted everyone with a smile. However, today was different, and she had to admit it to herself. This was the last week she would be working for KBW, and she had mixed emotions about it.

She honestly hated to leave the job, that not only was she good at, but she loved so well. However, she was excited about moving on to her new position at the City of Camden as Assistant City Planner.

When she reached her office, however, she was stunned to find everything had been removed.

She ran down the hall in search of her immediate Supervisor, Chris.

Gwen stopped her in the hall. "Hi, Randi."

"Hey, Gwen, is Chris in his office?"

"No. I was on my way to let you know that you have a meeting in the Conference Room," Gwen informed her.

Miranda took a deep breath and let it out. She threw up her hands and asked, "What, they're putting me out before my last day? And, where is my stuff?"

"Go to the Conference Room, Randi," Gwen said.

Miranda glared at her for a moment, "Conference Room?"

Gwen simply nodded her head, "After you."

Miranda turned and headed toward the Conference Room. When she walked in, she noticed a woman sitting at the head of the table she'd never seen before. Kyle was sitting beside her.

"Randi," Kyle stood as soon as he saw her.

"Ky– Mr. Waters, what's going on?"

The woman looked up at Miranda. "Hello, I'm Antoinette Waters, Vice-President of KBW. You must be Miranda Jones." She held out her hand and Miranda gave her a firm shake. "Please have a seat." She pointed to a chair across from Kyle.

No way could this be Kyle's mother, she thought. *The woman is much too young to have a thirty-year-old son.*

"Can I get you anything Mr. Waters?" Gwen asked.

"I'm fine, Gwen, thank you," he responded.

She turned to the women. "Ms. Waters, Ms. Jones?"

"I'm fine too, thanks," Miranda said.

Antoinette said, "Yes, you can, Gwen. Please call Christopher and let him know we are ready to start."

"Yes, ma'am." Gwen looked at Miranda and winked at her. There was a huge smile on her face.

Chris walked into the room. "Sorry, I had a call from the State about our Environmental Study for the Grace Project."

"How is that going?" Ms. Waters asked.

"Well, let me just say I need to jump through one more hoop before we can get it approved," Chris answered, "but it's not a problem at all," he added.

"Good." Ms. Waters turned to address Miranda. "Now that Christopher is here, we can get started. My guess is you don't know why you're here, Ms. Jones."

"No, I don't."

Reign 75

"Well, it's come to my attention by Christopher that KBW is about to lose one of the best technical designers we've had in years. Is that so?"

"I've accepted a job with the City of Camden."

"You know, Miranda," she said and then paused, "Is it all right if I call you Miranda?"

"Yes, that's fine," Miranda answered, wondering where this was going.

"I pride myself on keeping good employees and quickly getting rid of those who aren't team players. Christopher tells me you are a team player and I respect his opinion. He doesn't want to lose you."

Miranda looked at Chris as she answered, "Ms. Waters, he's expressed his feelings."

Ms. Waters stood and walked behind Kyle. "My brother here tells me he's talked to you and your mind is made up about leaving us."

Miranda looked Kyle in the eyes. "Yes, we've discussed it, and my last day is Friday."

"Well, that's why I'm here. I think what I have proposed will be to your liking." She moved back to her seat. "I'm here to offer you an increase in salary and a promotion. Christopher thinks you'll have no problem with becoming a Project Manager."

Miranda looked first at Chris, then at Kyle. She knew that Frank Farmer was supposed to be in line for the position after Dale Peters retired. As a matter of fact, there were three other people with more seniority than her in line for that position. "What about Mr. Farmer? He's always said that once Peters retired, he was next in line for that job."

"Farmer?" Ms. Water asked looking at Kyle.

"She's talking about Frank Farmer. You just moved him to the Harrisburg Office."

"Oh. No, he won't be in this office, and he's very happy about his promotion."

Miranda paused before saying, "I don't think I can handle the position at this time. I have something personal going on in my life and I know that it may interfere with such a demanding job."

Ms. Waters placed both her hands on the back of the chair she stood behind. "Oh, and what is it that would keep you from accepting my offer?" she asked.

"It's my mother. She's terminally ill, and just this past Friday, I found out the cancer she's been fighting for three years has spread and she doesn't have very much time left to live."

"Oh, I'm very sorry to hear that. However, I'm sure that you'll be able to take whatever time you need when the time comes to care for your mother."

"I've always worked with you when it comes to your mother, Randi, and you know that," Chris added.

Ms. Waters leaned over and pushed a package across the table to Miranda. "I'm sure that once you see what were offering you, you'll stay. Kyle, take Ms. Jones to her new office, please." She looked at Miranda. "We'll meet again on Friday after you've been able to absorb everything."

Kyle stood up and Miranda sat there for a moment in a daze. Kyle called her name to get her attention. Miranda slowly rose from her chair, picked up the package, and followed him. They quietly walked to what was to be her new office. Once there, Kyle closed the door and sat down in a guest chair across from the heavy oak desk. Miranda couldn't believe it. Someone had moved all her things to this new office. Standing there, she took a good look at her surroundings and then her eyes landed on Kyle.

He threw up his hands. "I know what you're thinking, but I swear I had nothing to do with this," Kyle defended. "Since I couldn't get you to stay, Chris called Toni."

"Toni?"

"My sister, Antoinette, the family calls her Toni. She likes to be called Antoinette when dealing in business."

"Oh."

"Well, aren't you going to open the envelope to see what she offered you?" Kyle seemed curious.

"It doesn't matter what the offer is," she answered. "Friday will be my last day here."

"Randi."

She interrupted him by holding up her hand. "My guess is your sister knows about us."

"No, I haven't said anything to her. My sister and I don't have that kind of relationship. The only person I told is my grandmother and that's because I wanted her opinion of you. Her opinion is the only one I care about, and she loves you."

Miranda smiled. She liked Kyle's grandmother very much. "What about Chris?"

"Chris knows that we went out a few times and that you decided not to go out with me anymore."

"Then, I'm sure Chris told your sister."

"No, I don't think so," he said, bemused. "Why are you concerned about that, anyway?"

"Because I can just imagine what the staff is thinking."

"What are they thinking, Randi? They don't know that I have any other interest in you other than as an employee."

"That's what you think. You don't know some of the people around here. I'm telling you the first thing that's going to be said is how does she get the promotion over Kevin or William when they've been here longer."

Kyle stood, "I'll tell you why they didn't get the job. It's because you've delivered every time, even under pressure, time and time again. Not to mention the Sixth Street Project where you saved Kevin's behind."

Miranda shot a look at him.

"What's the matter? You didn't think I knew about that?"

Miranda was dumbfounded.

"I know about that. I know about the Broad Street Project and how it got completed. I know about the Front Street Project and that it was you that redesigned the drawings so it could make the planning board meeting on time." Kyle walked to the door. "I may want you, but that's separate and apart from this company. I would never agree to a promotion of this magnitude without knowing it's deserved," he summarized.

Miranda didn't know what to say.

"I suggest you read the offer we've made you. And believe me when I say it's well deserved." He opened the door. "Have a great day, Ms. Jones." He softly closed the door behind him.

Miranda went around the desk and stumbled onto the chair. She couldn't believe he knew that she redesigned those drawings. That was supposed to have stayed between her and Chris. Miranda was never one to brag, she never had a need for pats on her back. She always gave the whole team credit, even when it was she who did the work. "I need to call Ivy," she whispered. But after she picked up the phone, she remembered that Ivy was in the mountains with Sheena helping her out of her depression.

There was a knock on the door. "Come in."

Gwen peep her head into the room. "Hey."

"Get in here, Gwen." She moved to the chair in front of her desk. "Sit your butt down." Gwen slid onto the chair. "You could have told me what was going on." Gwen looked at her with a half smile on her face. "Just a little warning would have been nice."

"And ruin the surprise? No way! Besides, you deserve this, Randi."

"Gwen, I've already accepted the job in Camden."

"So, call them and tell them you've changed your mind."

Miranda shook her head. "I need to leave, Gwen."

"Randi, this is the opportunity of a lifetime. Especially with you being a woman. There's never been a female in this position. And, you're good. You have an eye for details and because of you KBW has been awarded the Market Street Project."

Miranda had worked on the Market Street Designs for the last three months. They had been taken from Frank after the owner rejected his concept. Chris came to her asking if she could give the project a fresh prospective. No one told her that the project had been awarded. "I didn't know KBW got the project."

"We just found out late Friday afternoon. That's when Chris knew we couldn't afford to lose you. It's going to be announced at the staff meeting at ten. So be ready to be praised."

"I don't need praise. I only did what they pay me to do."

"I know, but every now and then it's nice to be recognized. Now, I had all your stuff dumped in here. But you let me know when you're ready, and I'll help you organize everything." She turned to leave and then stopped. "Oh, I was told to let you know that you can order whatever furniture you wanted and that I'll be your personal assistant." She turned to look at Miranda, who smiled back at her. "That's unless you'd rather have someone else."

Miranda dropped her head before looking up at Gwen again with a huge grin on her face. "If I stay, who would I want more than you?"

"Nobody, 'cause this promotion comes with a raise and I need it."

"I'd love to work with you. That's if I decide to stay. So please, Gwen, don't get your hopes up on the raise."

"Oh, you'll stay. I have a feeling they've made you an offer you can't refuse." Gwen practically skipped out of the room.

Miranda left the office late that evening. Just before leaving, she called her mother who told her to pick up some Chinese food for dinner since she didn't feel like cooking. After leaving the store, she called Jade and told her everything on her drive home. She needed someone else's opinion on the whole matter.

"So, you're saying that they almost tripled your salary and gave you an office with a window and a personal assistant to boot?" Jade asked for clarification.

"That's what I'm saying," Miranda confirmed.

"Is the job much different than what you were doing?"

"No, not really, I'm just over the whole department now. I'll be overseeing all the different projects going on."

"You love that. That's what you've always liked about this job. You've always said how you like seeing the design come from paper to life, did you not?"

"Yes, of course, but Kyle's family owns the company."

"Randi, you got the job before you ever met the man. You started going out with him before you knew his family owns KBW, and you had already fallen in love with Kyle before you knew what hit you."

"I'm not in love with him, so stop saying that."

"Oh, please! Right after you met that man, you told us how fine he was and how nice he treated you. If my memory serves me correctly, he even had that mechanic friend of his loan you a car while yours was being repaired. What mechanic do you know loans customers cars?" Jade paused. "And, you were buzzing around here grinning all the time until that crazy woman told you she was Kyle's ex-girlfriend. And, didn't you tell me that all of it was a misunderstanding?"

"Yes, but..."

"But nothing, you better get with the program, Rug Rat."

"What, oh now you're calling me a Rug Rat?"

"I call you that when you talk silly, Rug Rat."

"I'm hanging up on you."

"And, I'll come to your house and spank your tail. You can't be disrespecting your elders," Jade said while laughing.

Miranda was quiet. Serious.

"Are you still there?"

"Yes."

When she answered, Jade realized this was critical to Miranda. "Randi, you're going to have to lighten up. Stop trying to read into everything. Trust your instincts."

"That's the problem, Jade. I can't trust my instincts. Not when it comes to Kyle."

Jade knew then that Miranda had deeper feelings for Kyle than she made known. As far as she knew, this was the first time Miranda had affection for any man, so the advice had to be genuine. "Then trust the God in you."

Chapter Nine

Sheena was sitting in a rocking chair on the back porch when Bill walked over to her, offering her a cup of hot chocolate and a blanket. "It's chilly out here! I thought you might need something to warm you up."

"How thoughtful of you, Bill, thank you."

"You're welcome."

Sheena fixed her eyes on Bill, knowing that not only had she been set up to take this trip, but that Ivy had been set up as well.

Even though Bill had sat on a rocker next to Sheena and closed his eyes, he knew she was watching him. He turned to look at her to be sure and he was right. She smiled at him and continued to stare boldly.

"What?" Bill asked.

"I'm sure that it was you who came to Ivy with the idea to come here," Sheena assumed.

"Oh, you think this is my idea?" Bill looked dumbfounded.

"Uh-huh, you know, let's take Sheena up in the mountains and get her into some clear fresh air so we can drive her out of that depressed mood."

Bill knew their plan had been exposed and even though it wasn't his idea, he went along with her assumption. "So," Bill turned to look out into the darkness.

"Well, I think it's really sweet of all of you to do this just for little ol' me. But to get Ivy to pretend your relationship had reached another level shows me just how much she loves me and I think that's so precious."

"She's been worried about you and it's not just the attack, but other things."

Sheena knew he wasn't just talking about her depression. "I'm okay, Bill. Ivy doesn't have to worry about me."

"You do know they guarded you from one of your co-workers while you were in the hospital?"

"I don't have to guess who?"

Bill shook his head. "She and Jade got into a huge argument in the waiting room about you."

"I didn't know that." She blew a sigh.

"Well, I think if Jade had been a cussing woman, your friend Josephine would have gotten a good tongue lashing."

"Well, thank God she's not!"

"Your girl Randi wasn't any better. She's the one that had everyone thinking that Josephine had something to do with the attack."

Sheena frowned. "Why would she think that? Just because the woman is different doesn't mean she's violent."

"Randi said you told her that you'd been getting obscene phone calls for over a month before the attack."

"Oh, for heaven's sake!" Sheena exclaimed. "The only reason she knows that is because she called me right after I'd gotten three in a row, and when I answered the phone I didn't say hello. I hollered in the phone to stop calling my home. I explained to her about the calls and that I'd been getting them for weeks. I was upset, but if I had been thinking, I wouldn't have told her as much as I did. Too much information for Randi is dangerous – as you can see."

"Well, I guess Randi was putting two and two together and getting nine," Bill said and chuckled.

"I love my friends, and I think you know that. I told them not to worry about me because between me and the Lord, all my issues will be taken care of."

"I know, but for Ivy, it's more than sisterly friendship. It's like you, Jade, and Randi are her children."

Sheena smiled. "Ivy's always been that way. She's older than us and she's always been like the big sister. So, I hope our relationship doesn't offend you."

"No, but I do think she worries a little too much about you all, but please don't tell her I told you that."

Sheena smiled at him. "You haven't told her, have you?" she asked matter-of-factly.

"Told her what?"

"That you're in love with her and have been since the day you met her." Bill continued to stare into the darkness, so Sheena went on. "My guess is that you wanted to be alone with her without the kids, so I became the convenient excuse to get her to come to this beautiful mountain retreat."

"How many times have I told you that you need to keep some opinions to yourself?" He looked at her and there was no humor in his eyes.

"You know me, Bill. I'm opinionated by nature. So let's don't go there… again."

"I've told you that you need to keep your opinions to yourself," he snapped.

Sheena ignored his statement. "I think you need to just tell her. Just open your heart to her. The honesty and sincerity will flow."

Bill turned his head to look into the house. Ivy was standing near the kitchen sink loading the dishwasher and talking to Marshall who was sitting at the table.

"She keeps hinting that she's taking up too much of my time. She thinks I'm spending too much time with, quote - unquote, *her* children."

"Well, that's because you're still perpetrating a fraud."

Bill looked at Sheena. "I don't want to move too fast. You know how Ivy is. She wants to do everything decent and in order."

"Bill, she truly has no idea how you feel? Am I the only one who knows?"

"No, Marshall knows. He's known from the start, way before you figured it out."

"Well, even though she's my best friend, I never breathed a word. I promised you my lips were sealed ever since I figured it out in the limo the day of Ray's funeral. That was over two years ago." She met his eyes. "You need to tell her."

"You think enough time has passed for her to be ready to hear how I feel about her?"

"Bill, I think two years is more than enough time."

His mind went to Ivy's children who he adored. He smiled remembering the comment made by the girls. "The twins asked me to be their play daddy."

Sheena chuckled, "really?"

Bill nodded. "I told them that I loved them better than any play daddy could."

"That's nice, Bill. They really do love you. I hope you know that."

"I didn't think it possible, but I love them too. A few weeks ago, Ivy told me she didn't want me to take them for the weekend. She ordered me to spend some time alone and directed me to call one of my girlfriends and enjoy an adult weekend. So, I tried it… and I was miserable, to say the least."

Sheena knew about misery. "I know the feeling."

"I was bored with my date. She was tired of me talking about Ivy and the kids and told me so. It was bad, Sheen, it was really bad."

"You need to find the courage to just tell her."

"I know you're right."

"So, tell me, is Marshall a part of this plan too, or is he an innocent bystander like me?"

Bill smiled, thinking, *she hasn't figured out everything.* "No, Marshall just allowed us to use this place."

"I see. Well, it's almost seven, so I think I'll go and get ready to go to that surprise location you said you wanted to take us to." She stood and headed into the house.

"You're going to like it," Bill yelled to her retreating back.

"I understand that you're almost finished with your garden," Marshall was saying to Ivy as Sheena came in.

"Where are you going?" Ivy asked as Sheena passed through the kitchen.

"I think that chocolate went straight through me. I'll be back in a few."

"Minutes or hours?" Ivy asked jokingly as she laughed.

"Ha! Ha!" Sheena was taking the stairs two at a time.

"I told Bill he was making that chocolate too rich," Marshall joined Ivy in laughter.

"What were we talking about?" Ivy asked.

"Your garden masterpiece."

"Oh, yeah, I'd say a few more days and it will be complete. And, I think I've done better than any professional gardener could have done."

"I'm sure you have."

Ivy paused for a moment. "You know what? The house came out much better than I thought it would. And Bill has been so wonderful. He's dealt with all the contractors. He made sure not one of them got over on me. Everything was done decent and in order."

"Bill cares about you, Ivy," Marshall commented.

"I know. But I've been trying to tell him that he needs to take some time for himself. Do you know how much time he spends with me and my kids?"

"I don't think he'd be anywhere he doesn't want to be," Marshall remarked before biting into an apple.

Ivy looked toward the stairs and lowered her voice, not wanting Sheena to overhear their conversation. "The kids have gotten so attached to him. I'm afraid that once he does meet someone and begins to date, my kids are going to feel rejected."

The answer came from the doorway. "That will never happen." Bill came into the kitchen and joined Marshall at the table.

Ivy turned her back to them, attending to the dishes in the sink. "You never know what the future holds."

"I know I would never hurt your children, Ivy," Bill was adamant.

"I'd be the first to say you wouldn't mean to hurt them. You of all people know they've been through so much and..." Ivy stopped mid-sentence and turned to look directly at him with her hand on her hip. "Besides, you deserve to have a life other than me and my rug rats. I'm not a fool." She stopped again and looked toward the stairs and whispered, "Enough about that, I need to tell you this before she comes back down here." She moved closer to the table. "I got a phone call from my father earlier today. He said Jason called him."

"Jason?" Marshall was surprised.

Ivy nodded. "He said Jason told him that he's been trying to get in touch with Sheena for two weeks."

"I'm sure she's going to be glad to here that." Ivy could hear the disappointment and pain in Marshall's voice.

"I talked to her mother. She said she talked to Jason and asked him not to call her home anymore."

"She's in love with him, Ivy. It's probably best that she try and work things out with him," Marshall said flatly.

"You know what, Marshall; I would say I agree with you if I hadn't called that flat-footed weasel when she was first admitted into the hospital."

"You called him?"

"Yes, I thought he should know. But before I could even tell him what was going on he said, if you're calling to tell me something about Sheena, I don't want to hear it. We are through. It's over and I'm done with her. Quote, unquote."

"Wow!" Marshall exclaimed.

"I didn't just leave it there," Ivy went on. "I remember saying to him, Jason you don't understand. By the time that came out of my mouth, he just about yelled at me and said no Ivy, *you* don't understand. It's over. I could care less what's going on with her and he hung up on me."

"So, he never really knew…"

"Like hell he didn't. He works for the Department of Education, same as she does. I'm sure some type of memo or something went out. So, don't try to make any excuses for him, Marshall."

"But they work in different offices. He may not have known until now what happened."

"Well, I have nothing to say to him. Her mother and father have nothing to say to him. He said it was over, so let it be over," Ivy said with finality.

"So you all really aren't going to tell her?"

"I guess since he's called my father to intervene, we'll have to tell her at some point. But, I'm not saying anything until we leave this mountain. So, don't say a word about what I just told the two of you."

Bill whispered, "She's coming down the steps now." They all became quiet.

Sheena pulled out a chair next to Marshall. "Okay, I missed you and Marshall talking about your garden. Did you ever get that gazebo you wanted?"

"Oh, that's right. You haven't been to the house in months."

Sheena reached into the bowl of fruit and removed a grape. "Well, I was a little tied up," she said with the fruit in her mouth.

They all laughed.

"That's an understatement! But to answer your question, yes, the gazebo is installed." Then Ivy directed her attention to Bill. "Are we still going to this café you said you found?"

"Yes, I'd like to leave around nine."

"Wonderful! I can't wait to see where you're taking us."

Chapter Ten

For the first time, Sheena wished she knew how to dance. Ivy was out there on the floor with Bill swinging to the music of the live band.

"I'm beginning to feel neglected," Marshall said and pouted.

Sheena turned to him with the most serious look on her face. "Why?"

"Because you won't dance with me."

"Marshall, if I knew how to dance, I would. Believe me, it's not because I don't want to. I just don't want to embarrass you or myself," she answered.

"You're joking, you can't dance?"

Sheena shook her head. "Not a step."

"Come on, Sheena."

"I'm serious. I've tried to dance and I just look silly. My mother told me I look like a chicken having an epileptic fit," she said jokingly.

Marshall laughed after he watched her gyrated her body in her chair to demonstrate how she looked. "Well, I'll tell you what, when the next slow song is played, I'll lead you to the dance floor and into a slow easy progression." He waited for her to agree.

At that moment, Sheena realized she liked Marshall. He was easy to be around and she felt comfortable talking with him. She and Marshall had never spent any time together other than professionally. Now she was seeing another side to him, and she liked what she saw.

Marshall smiled at her, waiting on her answer. She smiled back and nodded her head.

She looked out into the crowd in search of Ivy. There she was with Bill circling her as they danced. She knew her friend was truly enjoying herself. She hadn't seen Ivy this happy in a long time and for an instant, she felt a hint of jealousy. She wanted to be happy, too. She wanted someone to have feelings for her as she knew Bill did for Ivy.

"This song is for us," Marshall rose and took her by the hand and led her onto the dance floor. Like magic, they easily swayed to the music of *Always and Forever*, a song made popular by a group called Heat Wave long ago. She didn't utter a word as she concentrated on their movements – which, to her surprise, came without difficulty. "See, you were wrong about yourself, you have rhythm," he whispered sweetly in her ear.

After his breath sent a shiver down her spine, she lifted her head, meeting his direct gaze. At that very moment, something gripped her and a feeling like no other came over her. Sheena knew she was too inexperienced to try and interpret what had just happened, so she laid her head on his shoulder and concentrated on becoming one with him in the dance.

Marshall stroked her back with as much affection as a man could show a woman publicly. He knew she felt what he had communicated to her with his eyes. He knew at that very moment she was analyzing what had just transpired between the two of them. "When we get back home, I want us to continue to see each other."

Sheena lifted her head from his shoulder and met his gaze prepared to protest, but "I'd like that," came out instead.

Marshall smiled and pulled her as close as he could to him and then the song ended much too quickly.

He led her back to the table. Ivy and Bill were grinning at them as they approached. "I thought you didn't dance," Bill pointed out.

Sheena smiled modestly. "Well, I do now."

Before Sheena could take a seat, Ivy stood up. "Come with me, Sheena, I need to freshen up."

They weaved their way through the crowd and when they reached the corridor, Sheena said, "you really were kicking your heels up out there, girl."

"I'm really having a wonderful time."

"Oh, I can tell. I haven't seen you this jubilant in a long time." Sheena pushed open the restroom door.

"I was so shocked to see you on the dance floor. I had to pinch myself to be sure I wasn't dreaming!"

"If I hadn't felt an instant of jealousy, I probably wouldn't have tried it. Besides, why should you have all the fun?"

Ivy eyed her friend with a smile as she dabbed the makeup from her face with a tissue while looking in the mirror. "You probably haven't recognized it yet, but Marshall is sweet on you, girl."

"Yeah, I know. But, I wasn't sure until we danced."

Ivy stopped moving and stared at Sheena's reflection in the mirror. "He told you?"

"No, I saw it in his eyes." She paused and Ivy waited, not wanting to interrupt her thoughts. "Ivy, it's something I saw in his eyes that I just can't explain. But when we danced, I felt it too. To be honest, I wasn't sure what I was experiencing, and then as if he knew I needed confirmation, he said he wanted us to see each other when we got back home."

"Get out of here!" Ivy turned to face her with her mouth agape. "So – are you?"

"Yes, I like Marshall. I like talking to him and he's easy to be with."

"Oh, thank you, Jesus," Ivy prayed.

"Why are you thanking the Lord?"

"Girl, I've been praying hard for you, and you know why."

"Jason?"

"No, not just Jason. I've been praying about everything you've been going through since you befriended Josephine."

"Oh. Well, it's like Jason said. I just need to know I can trust a man, that's all. I think I can trust Marshall. I've been acquainted with him long enough to take a chance don't you think."

"Oh, most definitely."

"Besides, I've been honest with him about my feelings. We've talked enough so I think we have an understanding."

Sheena was leaning against the wall as she spoke and what she was saying was like music to Ivy's ears. "See, now aren't you glad I didn't let you go home after the first night we were here?

"Yes, Ivy. I'm glad we stayed."

Chapter Eleven

Miranda sat at the desk in her bedroom and read the proposal five times before it thoroughly sank in. At the salary they quoted, she would be a fool to not accept the position for doing a job she loved so much. She wanted to call Kyle to apologize for the comment she'd made earlier in her office. That had been the first time he'd really been upset with her. However, she figured she'd give him time to cool off before she talked to him.

She positioned the document neatly on her desk as she thought about the phone call she'd received from Jason less than a half hour ago.

She picked up her phone and dialed.

"Hello…"

"Stop that!" She could hear Jade's husband in the background.

Miranda grimaced. "I caught you and Darrell at a bad time."

"No, it's all right."

"Hang up the phone," she heard Darrell say. "She'll call you back tomorrow, Mom."

"It's not your mother, now stop," Jade ordered him.

"I'll call you tomorrow."

"No, Randi, it's fine. You sound funny, you okay?"

"Jason called me."

"Oh, my goodness, he called me too! Did you tell him anything?"

"I told him Sheena was out of town."

"So did I. He wanted me to give him her new cell number."

"He asked me for it too," Miranda replied. "I told him I couldn't give it to him and that he needed to get it from her."

"Have you talked to Ivy?"

"No. Have you?"

"No, but he told me he was going to call Pastor Jones," Jade informed her friend. "So let's face it, if he did that, then I know he's called Ivy."

"You're probably right. You know, he wanted to know how she was doing and I told him she was fine now after being in the hospital for almost a month." Miranda sighed. "I know I added insult to injury when I told him she was in critical care for seven days while in and out of consciousness."

"I asked him why he didn't call her while she was in the hospital and he said he didn't know," Jade added.

"He told me the same thing."

"I know for a fact that Ivy called him the day it happened and tried to tell him what was going on, Randi."

"I know, and I told him so. He said he was upset at the time and that he had really made up in his mind that he wanted to forget her. He said they had agreed they wouldn't contact each other anymore."

"Well, I think he should continue that same train of thought. Like you said, the man is Muslim. He needs to just leave her alone and let her move on with her life."

"Well, in all honesty, if I had to make a choice, I'd rather her marry a Muslim than be with Josephine and her crew," Miranda remarked.

Jade's voice carried conviction. "Sheena's going to be just fine. Josephine has only seen her a few times since the attack and, to be honest with you, I haven't seen anything out of the ordinary going on between them. Josephine knows the deal. I'm sure of it. Now Jason, on the other hand, could be a problem."

"I agree. Maybe we should call Ivy and warn her."

"I'll do a three-way call," Jade offered. "Hold on."

Miranda waited while Jade connected them to Ivy's cell. Her mind went back to Kyle. She understood that love was unpredictable. It had not been her desire to fall for Kyle. She was attracted to him the moment she saw him. The man was gorgeous, and she was far too attracted to him to be around him every day of the week. Taking that job would mean just that. Being around him on Monday, Tuesday, Wednesday, Thursday, Friday and some Saturdays, and date him too…. Oh, my God. "There ain't no way!" She spoke the thought out loud.

"There ain't no way for what?" Jade asked.

"There ain't no way we're going to let Jason back in Sheena's life," Miranda answered.

"Hey, Randi," Ivy yelled over the noisy background.

"Hey, Ivy!"

"What's up, ladies?"

"Where are you?" Miranda wanted to know.

"Turn the music down for a minute so you can hear us," Jade ordered.

"I can't turn the music down. We're at a café where they have a live band."

"Ivy Jones Miller, I know you're not out in some club somewhere hanging out with the heathens," Miranda chastised.

"See, that's your main problem, Rug Rat. You're always judging people. So just shut up and tell me why you all are bothering me while me and Sheena are here getting our groove on."

"I was just about to ask you where she was," Jade said.

"She's on the dance floor with Marshall. She just found out he's sweet on her."

"Sheena is dancing?" both women exclaimed almost in unison.

"I wouldn't have believed it myself if I didn't see it with my own eyes. But Marshall has her out there on the floor swaying to the music."

"What?" Jade couldn't believe her ears.

"You're not joking?" Miranda asked. "She's really dancing in public?"

"Yes, yes, yes, and look, let me call you all back later."

Jade rushed in. "Wait, we need to tell you something... Jason called us today. He's trying to get in touch with Sheena."

"I figured he'd call one of you."

"Oh, so you know?"

"Yes. You didn't give him any information, did you?"

"I didn't breathe a word," Miranda answered.

"Neither did I."

"Good, we'll deal with it when we get back home. Right now, she's laughing and enjoying herself and I don't want to bring her down with talk about Jason."

"Okay. You'll be home on Sunday, right?" Jade asked to confirm.

"That's the plan."

"Oh, Ivy?"

"Yeah."

"He did say he was coming to Philly next week," Jade said.

"Okay, we'll deal with it when we get back."

Jade and Miranda talked a few more minutes about her job offer before hanging up. Miranda's mother waited until she was off the phone to add her own opinion. "It's not right to hold information from Sheena, Miranda."

"I know, Mama. It's just that he's turned his back on her when she was at her lowest, and I'm really disappointed in him about that."

"It still doesn't make it right."

"Her mother is the one who hasn't told her he's called. I only found out he's been trying to contact her after he called me today. Besides, Ivy said she'll tell her when they get back from the mountains."

Her mother nodded. "Okay. Goodnight, sweetheart."

"Goodnight, Mama." She kissed her cheek as the phone rang. "Hello?"

"Hi, Randi."

Miranda felt her heart do flips. "Kyle." His name came out brokenly.

His voice was warm, but his words were all business. "Did you read the proposal?"

She was immediately disappointed. "Yes, I read it."

"And...?"

She tried to keep her voice even. "I'm praying on it."

"Praying?"

What part of prayer don't you understand? "Yes, Kyle. I'm praying about it," she said clearly.

"Randi, you will not get a better deal anywhere in the city or the surrounding area."

"That may be so, but money isn't everything," she snapped. Kyle was silent. It took a few moments for her to realize there would be no verbal fencing. Miranda swallowed her pride. "Look, I'm sorry." She was frustrated with not knowing how to deal with him. "It seems I've been on the defensive with you and I shouldn't be. I should be grateful that Chris recognized a good employee and took the initiative to bring it to your attention."

"Thank you, Randi. 'Cause I really don't want to argue with you. I genuinely like you. You have all the qualities I want in a woman which includes your defensiveness."

"Kyle..."

"Let me finish... Like I told you earlier, your job has nothing to do with how I feel about you. You're good at what you do and KBW needs your talent. However, if you think you can't work for my family and be my woman, then you need to take that job at the City of Camden."

Miranda blew out a sigh and leaned against her headboard. "I understand."

"Do you really understand?"

"Yes," she said softly.

"Just remember this. You were working for my family before you knew I was a part of the family, and you and I had no problems about my family background until you found out who my parents were."

"You deceived me, Kyle. You should have told me who you were. You should have been upfront about everything."

"I wanted you to like me for me, not where I came from or who my family was," he said and chuckled, "but who would have ever thought that you'd reject me because I'm the boss's son?"

"I'm not rejecting you. It's just that we started off with deception. It's like you didn't trust me."

"I didn't know you, Randi. I've been in relationships before and it takes time for me to trust someone. It was never personally against you." There was a long pause.

"I think... it's best for all concerned... that I leave."

"Are you sure?"

She took a deep breath before replying. "Yes, I'm sure."

"Okay," he said, and she could hear something she couldn't identify in his voice. "Chris is going to be disappointed, and so is Toni. She's been bragging about the offer she made you. She told my father that it was an offer she knew you wouldn't be able to refuse."

"Apologize to her for me."

"No, you'll have to do that yourself. We have dinner with my family on Friday night."

"Excuse me?" Miranda was clearly surprised at his remark.

"You heard me, we have dinner at The Pub in Pennsauken with my family on Friday night."

"Kyle, I can't."

"Why, you have something else to do?"

"Yes, I'm going to church."

"You can't cancel one service to have dinner with my family?"

"Why would you want me to have dinner with your family? Is it to twist my arm about taking your job offer?" She spat the words out.

Again, Kyle was silent. After a full minute Miranda whispered, "I have to go."

"Don't hang up on me," he warned.

"I need to hang up."

"If you hang the phone up, I promise you I'm coming to your house tonight and tell your mother how you're treating me."

"You wouldn't."

"Try me."

Miranda knew he was serious, so she didn't try him.

"See, I had a feeling you didn't understand. I said if you had a problem with dating me and working for my family, then leave. So since you've decided to leave KBW, I'm fine with that. I don't like it, but I can live with it. But as for you and me, we're still seeing each other."

"Who do you think you are to tell me what I'm going to do?"

"I'm a man who's found a rare jewel and I don't want to lose it." Kyle waited for her response.

Miranda dropped the hand that held the phone to her lap. She couldn't believe he just said that. She switched the receiver to her other ear. She took a deep breath and said, "Kyle, I'm begging you. Please don't play games with me. I'm vulnerable right now and I just don't have the strength to guard myself."

"You don't have to safeguard yourself against me. I have never met anyone like you before. If anything, I should have protected myself from you. Do you really think my intentions were to fall for you when I met you on the highway in that old broken-down Ford LTD?"

Miranda shook her head as if he could see her.

"I never had to beg a woman to go out with me. Here I am chasing behind you like a dog in heat. If any other woman possessed this power, do you think she'd reject it like you are?"

Miranda didn't know how to respond – or even whether she should respond.

Kyle pressed, "The truth of the matter is, I can truly envision a future with you, and there is no other woman that's made me feel that way before."

Miranda let out a deep breath before she realized she'd been holding it. She was stunned at his admission. "What time?"

"What?"

"What time on Friday?"

"I'll pick you up at seven."

Chapter Twelve

It was eight in the morning when Sheena heard Ivy leave her room to go downstairs to the kitchen. Sheena was a terrible cook and everyone who knew her knew it. This morning she was going to put an end to that reputation using what she had learned since secretly taking cooking lessons at the local community college.

"Hey."

Ivy was surprised. "You're up early, Ms. Dancing Machine. Good morning!"

"Oh, you have some nerve. I had three dances. All slow, mind you. But you, Miss Real Dancing Machine, missed the only three dances I did. And, if you weren't so busy staring at me dancing you wouldn't have missed those."

"Oh, okay, you got jokes this morning."

"You were no joke on the dance floor. I'm signing you and Bill up for Soul Train."

"I'm not talking about the dance floor, Ms. Thing. You just put on an apron. What do you think you're about to do?"

"I'm going to cook breakfast this morning. You can watch me."

"Uh, Sheena, baby, you don't know how to cook, remember?"

"You sit, I'm cooking this morning."

Ivy grinned. "Oh, I know for sure now that you lost some of your memory when you were hit on the head." She attempted to take the apron from Sheena.

"No, Ivy. Let me show you. I can do this, I've been practicing. You set the table and let me handle the rest."

When the men came downstairs, the food was on the table and Ivy was amazed. Sheena had made home-fried potatoes, ham and cheese omelets, and cheese toast.

"I'm impressed!" Ivy looked at the food in astonishment. Sheena smiled from ear to ear. "Now, I pray it tastes as good as it looks."

"I know it's good," Marshall assured. Then, he prayed.

The food was better than it looked and Sheena couldn't have been more proud of herself. The last time Jason teased her about her non-cooking skills, she enrolled herself into cooking classes. For almost a year, once a week, every Monday night, she'd gone to class to learn the art of cooking.

"It looks like Sheena's been holding back on you, Ivy. She can indeed cook," Bill complimented her.

"The men will handle the dishes. You ladies get ready to go horseback riding," Marshall said.

"Horseback riding? I can't ride a horse. I've never been on a horse in my life," Sheena protested.

"Well, there's a first time for everything."

༄༅

It was well in the afternoon when they arrived back from the stables. Sheena knew that when morning came, she was going to be stiff and sore.

"That was fun," Ivy said as she rubbed her hip. "I know I'm going to pay for it in the morning though."

"Me too," Sheena answered.

Ivy peered at her. "You and Marshall got lost for a while, where did you two go?"

"We took the path by the river. Marshall figured you and Bill needed to be alone."

"I think Marshall wanted to be alone with *you*."

Sheena giggled. "I'm sure you're right."

"I've really gotten to know him a little better and I like the casual side of him."

"I do, too. He's real easy to talk to." Sheena paused and looked Ivy directly in the eyes. "You know, I think I probably shared some things with him I shouldn't have."

"Really, like what?"

"Stuff about Jason and... well... just a lot of stuff... too much... I felt too comfortable with him."

"Well, I think you being able to talk to him so freely is a good thing."

"Maybe you're right. He told me I need to be true to myself."

Ivy narrowed her eyes. "Aren't you true to yourself?"

"No," Sheena admitted. "I've been hiding behind my career, my faith, my education; and never just being me."

"But all that makes you who you are." Ivy saw Sheena drop her head. "Okay, just so you'll know, I've been concerned about you; and it's not just me concerned, but everyone who loves you. That's one of the reasons why I wanted to get you here to this place so you could relax and maybe talk about anything that's been bothering you. So, tell me what's on your mind Sheena."

"I really wish I could. But I know you. You'll judge me."

"Is that what I do?"

"Yes, you'll act like you're listening, but then you'll get on the phone and call Randi and then Randi will call

Jade; and the next thing I know I'll be called to your house for a girl's night out, but I'll be the topic of conversation."

"I think you're exaggerating a bit."

"Oh, really, then who was it that called Jason and told him about my being confused about my sexuality?"

"Sheena…"

"You told him what I'd told you in private."

"Sheena, it wasn't like that."

"Really, then how was it, Ivy?"

Ivy blew out a sigh. "How did we get on this conversation?"

"I needed him, Ivy. I needed him to come and see me. Why didn't you tell him that?"

Ivy threw up her hands. "Okay, you want the truth? I tried to tell him. I called him from the hospital hours after you were brought in. He didn't want to talk to me." Ivy blew out her breath in frustration. "I really didn't want to tell you this now but – let me tell you exactly what happened. When we got to the hospital we found your parents………..

"What happened?" All the girls asked almost in unison when they reached the area where Sheena's parents had been waiting after speaking to the doctor about her condition. Mr. Daniels answered because his wife was too upset to even speak at the moment. "The police said it wasn't an accident. They said she was beaten."

"Oh, my God! Who would want to hurt her?" Miranda asked.

"That's what the police asked us. I don't know anyone who hates her so much they would want to beat her the way they say she's been beaten."

"It's pretty bad?" Jade asked.

"They just took her up to surgery. The doctor said they have to relieve the pressure on her brain."

All the girls gasped. Jade broke down in tears.

It took Ivy only a moment to know what they had to do. "No!" she shouted. Everyone looked at her. "We don't have time to cry and feel sorry. It's time to pray," Ivy said, wiping her eyes.

"You're right. She's in surgery and we have to be vigilant. We're in spiritual warfare."

Ivy grasped Mr. Daniels' hand. He took his wife's hand. Jade grasped Mrs. Daniels' hand and Miranda's with the other, forming a circle. Pastor Jones and his wife walked in the room just in time to join the circle for prayer.

After they prayed they lingered in the hospital waiting for more news of her condition. After about an hour, Ivy pulled her cell phone from her purse.

"I'm going to call Jason," she said to Jade who was sitting next to her. "He should know what's going on."

"I agree." Ivy and Jade walked over to the window. Ivy paged through her contact index searching for Jason's number, which was programmed in her phone from the last time she contacted him a week ago. She dialed the number.

He answered on the second ring, "Hello."

"Jason?"

"Yes."

"It's Ivy."

Immediately he snapped, "Ivy, I don't want to hear anything about your friend, okay? She and I parted ways for good and I'd like to leave it that way."

"But..."

"There's no if, ands, or buts about it. We are through. I don't want to know anything about her, so don't call me for any reason at all concerning her."

Ivy couldn't believe her ears. "But you don't understand, she was in an accident," she whispered as loudly as she could. But how could he hear even if she screamed it since he was talking over her words.

"What's he saying?" Jade was curious, especially since Ivy had a look of awe on her face.

"Jason." Ivy called as loud as she could without bringing notice to herself. "Hold on. Let me go outside..."

"I'm sorry, Ivy, but I have to move on with my life and I can't allow her to consume me anymore." Ivy was headed to the exit door with Jade and Miranda following when she heard him say, "It's over, so please, don't call me and tell me anything about her." Then without warning, he disconnected.

"Oh, no he didn't." Ivy was appalled.

"What's going on?" Jade asked again.

"He hung up on me." Ivy redialed his number. "I can't believe him. He didn't even try to listen to what I had to say."

"He hung up on you?" Jade wanted confirmation.

Ivy nodded her head. "He said he didn't want to hear anything about Sheena."

"What?" Miranda gasped.

"Answer the phone, Jason." Ivy said into the phone.

The automated message center picked up. "The party that you are trying to reach is not available at this time and the mailbox is full. To page this person, press three." Ivy pressed three. "If the number you are calling from is the number you can be reached, please press pound." Ivy did that. "Your message has been sent. Good bye."

Ivy looked at her friend. "I really tried to call him, Sheena. He never called me back and I tried to call him again that evening and the next day too. His box was full, so I couldn't leave a message, but I paged him every time." Ivy saw the look of devastation on Sheena's face. Her eyes welled up and she hated herself for telling her friend what Jason had said. "If there's any consolation, he called your mother for the first time about two weeks ago. He asked her how you were doing."

"But, he never came to see me," Sheena said just above a whisper.

"He wanted to come see you, but your mother told him not to. Maybe she should have…"

"All this time and he just called two weeks ago?" Sheena interrupted Ivy to ask.

Ivy nodded silently.

"Then, she told him right. She did what was best for me." She wiped the tears from her eyes and straightened her spine as she moved to the window to look out into the darkness. "He was right, Ivy. It's over between us. He told me he didn't want me to call him, and I need to get it through my head that we aren't even friends anymore."

Ivy leaned against the dresser. "So, you're okay with this?"

"Yes, I need to move on. I need to make my own happiness." Sheena moved to sit on the bed. "I'm going to take Vincent's advice," she said and began to untie her sneakers

"Vincent?" Ivy questioned.

"He asked me not to call him Marshall. He wants me to call him by his first name," Sheena glanced over at Ivy and gave a weak smile.

"Oh…."

"I've been talking to Marshall – I mean Vincent – about everything. He's a good listener and he hasn't judged me either."

"Well, that's good. And I promise, from now on I'll be more careful and I won't judge you either."

"You won't judge me?"

"I won't. I promise."

Sheena sighed. "Then, I can tell you that I'm going to seek some professional help once we get back home. Something is seriously wrong with me, Ivy, and I need therapy." Sheena waited for a reaction from her.

"Would I be judging if I said there's nothing wrong with you?"

Sheena laughed. "I see now it's going to take some work. But you know, I still love you, Miss Know-It-All."

Ivy smiled. "You know I never meant to do you any harm."

"I know, that's why I love you." Sheena pulled her knees to her chest. "I'm starting to really feel the soreness from that saddle."

"I'm thinking about sitting in the tub for a while. Maybe you should do the same."

"Good idea. I think I will."

Ivy turned to leave and Sheena called to her. "Ivy, did you know that in some countries, marriage proposals by contract are real?"

Ivy turned back to look at Sheena. "I've heard, but not in modern-day society."

"Then what's a prenuptial agreement?"

Ivy folded her arms and leaned against the door jamb. "Okay, you and Marshall were joking about this the other day, at least I assumed you were joking."

"Marshall... I mean Vincent and I were just thinking about how nice it could be. I mean we both know what we're getting into. We both know we don't love each other, but we do like and respect each other, and you never know. Some couples have less to build on and what we have could grow into love."

"Vincent has had a crush on you for some time while you've been infatuated with Jason. So how could you even think about a proposal from him?" Ivy paused. "I'm not judging, mind you."

"But it's making a choice with my mind and not my feelings or my heart. I trust my mind more so than what I feel in my heart," Sheena argued.

"Love is an important component in a marriage, Sheena. Believe me, I know."

"No disrespect, Ivy, but you loved Ray. Even though you loved him, if he hadn't died, don't you agree that you would have probably divorced him?" Ivy stared at Sheena for a moment and she knew Ivy was pondering her question.

"Yes, I probably would have," Ivy finally answered.

"So in the words of Tina Turner, what does love have to do with it?"

"Real love has everything to do with it."

"But who really knows what real love is, Ivy? You said to me yourself that you didn't know if I really loved Jason. I've thought about that and I've concluded that you were right. I was being driven by emotions and not real love. I'm emotionally attached to Jason. I've never allowed another man to get that close to me and I really want to. I can make that choice, can't I?"

"Yes, you have that control."

"Vincent reminded me today that according to the Bible, it's a man that finds a wife."

"I think he's moving a little too fast."

"Now you're judging."

Ivy threw up her hands, "Okay, you're right. That was judging."

"I have the faith that I will be totally and completely happy one day. But faith without works is dead, right?"

"Yes, you're right. Are you coming back downstairs?" Ivy asked.

"Maybe after I take a soak in the tub," she said, rubbing her thighs. "I feel the pain coming on."

Chapter Thirteen

"Don't let my son intimidate you," Grand Waters whispered to Miranda as the waiter served their drinks. "You are a lovely young woman, so just be yourself."

Kyle had grasped Miranda's hand beneath the table and Grand Waters had to know that she was now holding it almost in a grip lock. Intimidation was not only felt coming from her son, Kyle Waters the third, but from her granddaughter as well. If the dictionary had a picture of uppity, Antoinette Waters' face would be next to the description.

For the first time in her life, Miranda was uncomfortable and unsure of herself. His family was watching her as if they were trying to figure out everything about her with their eyes. She had been examined from head to toe.

"Your hair is lovely," Kyle's mother commented.

She had twisted her dreads together so that they laid all together down her back which had a French roll effect. "Thank you."

"How long did it take for it to grow like that?" She asked.

"I've been natural for about five years now."

"Well, it's beautiful."

Miranda was glad she approved. And, she was able to relax just a little more.

Miranda had met Kyle's grandmother a week after they started seeing each other and she enjoyed her company. She thanked God for his grandmother because, if it hadn't been for her, she probably would have made some excuse and left the table minutes after arriving.

Midway through the meal, Miranda was finally cozy enough to laugh freely at the stories Kyle's grandmother revealed about his childhood antics. "You know, Miranda, Kyle wanted to be a super hero when he was about four…"

"Come on, Grand, you're embarrassing me - enough already."

She waved her hand at him. "I purchased some superman pajamas for the boy and he wore them until they were too small for him to put on. You remember that, Kyle?"

"How can I forget?" He grinned at the memory.

Kyle's mother changed the conversation. "Miranda, Kyle tells us that your mother is ill."

"Yes, she's been battling cancer for some time now."

Her voice turned gentle. "What's her prognosis, if you don't mind me asking?"

"We just found out that they've done all they can do. She's in the hands of the Lord now."

"I'm so sorry to hear that. I'll keep your mother in my prayers."

"Thank you," Miranda whispered.

"What about your father?" Kyle's father asked her.

She cleared her throat, taken aback by the interrogation. "He died about five years ago."

"Miranda's father was the Pastor of Little Rock in Camden, and her grandfather was the Pastor of Cathedral of Faith," Grand Waters added.

"You knew her father, Mama?" Kyle's father asked.

"No, I met her grandfather a few years before he passed away."

"You never told me that," Kyle exclaimed with surprise.

Miranda was surprised to know she'd met her grandfather and had never mentioned it to her. There was an explanation. "That's because I hadn't connected Miranda to Pastor Jones until a week ago after I was talking to Pastor Murphy's wife. I was telling her about the wonderful girl my grandson met, and of course, she wanted to know exactly who she was. When I gave her Miranda's name she asked me if she wears dreadlocks and I told her yes. She told me that I'd met her grandfather years ago and she put it all together for me." She turned to Miranda. "Your father had a twin brother didn't he?"

"Yes, identical. Uncle James is the Pastor of Cathedral now."

"Reverend James Jones is your uncle?" Kyle's mother asked for clarification.

"Yes."

"Then your cousin was Ray Miller," Kyle's father said, nodding.

"No, Ray was married to my cousin, Ivy. My Uncle James is her father."

"It's my understanding you've entered into the ministry as well," Grand Waters said, helping herself to a roll.

"Wow, your friend really is informative. As a matter of fact, yes, I start seminary this fall," Miranda answered.

Kyle's mouth dropped. He knew then that he had much to learn about the woman who captivated him.

Toni dropped her napkin onto her plate. She had clearly had enough of the pleasantries. "Why didn't you accept my offer, Miranda?"

Kyle quickly turned to his sister. "Toni, I told you no business tonight," he reminded her.

"That was an offer of a lifetime, and I want to know why she didn't accept it."

Miranda knew she was going to have to deal with Kyle's sister tonight. She bowed her head for a moment in silent prayer.

"Toni, you are so wrong," Kyle said between clinched teeth.

Miranda tried to choose her words wisely. "I didn't accept your offer, because I want to move in another area. That offer simply confines me."

"What do you want, the Vice Presidency? I made you a Director, for Christ's sake!"

"Toni, this is not the time or the place," Kyle scolded her harshly.

"I'm about to lose a five-million-dollar contract because you insist on sleeping with the employees, and now you're telling me this isn't the time or…."

"Enough!" Grand Waters' voice cut through everything.

Miranda stood up. "I should go. It's been nice meeting you all."

Then Kyle stood up too. "Thanks, Toni," he said, his voice laced with sarcasm.

Miranda tucked her bag under her arm. "Enjoy the rest of your evening."

"Miranda, please don't leave," Mrs. Waters rushed in. "My daughter has a bad habit of speaking before she thinks."

"It's best I leave, Mrs. Waters, before I say something I shouldn't."

Grand Waters stood up and took Miranda by the hand. "Kyle, you sit. I need to speak with Miranda alone."

She led her by the hand to the restroom. There was one woman there washing her hands. Grand Waters waited until she left before she spoke. "Toni was just given the responsibility of running the company. She's a little high-strung and sometimes overbearing, but she's been able to keep the company out of the red. You see, my son was going to close the business after he'd been in that accident about four years ago. Mismanagement had KBW on its knees. Toni brought in Chris, and Chris brought in you. After that, things smoothed out and because of Chris' managerial skills and your innovative mind, the company began to attract new clients looking for fresh ideas. She doesn't want to lose you, Miranda."

Miranda looked at Grand Waters with a direct stare. "I'm not sleeping with your grandson. I'm saved and there's no way I could do that."

Grand Waters gave Miranda a tight hug. "I knew that without you telling me."

"I told Kyle that that was exactly what people would think if I got this promotion."

"Miranda, a lot of the people that work with you know that you're a large part of the success that KBW has enjoyed for the past few years. From the look on your face, it seems like you're the only one that doesn't know."

"It's been hard working for KBW. With my mother's illness and me having to take off so much time…"

"But, I was told you still get the job done in spite of your personal dilemmas."

The bathroom door opened and in came Toni. For an instant, her eyes locked with Miranda's.

Miranda stepped around Toni to get to the exit. "Pardon me, Grand Waters, we'll finish our conversation another time." Just when she moved to open the door she heard Toni speak, "Miranda, please forgive me. My mother is right. Sometimes I do speak before I think." She put out her hand. "Please."

Miranda had to be Christian enough to accept her apology since she was woman enough to give it. She shook her hand with a lot of speculation. "I'm not sleeping with your brother."

"Yes, I know. My brother just tore into me about that, too."

Miranda looked over at Grand Waters who was smiling.

Toni was quick to say, "Look, I'm in a jam and the truth is, we can't afford to lose you right now. With your talent, I know there'll be more opportunities for you with KBW. But, I don't want our competitors gaining from your talent."

"The City of Camden is not your competitor."

"But there'll be other offers and I know you won't be a city employee long."

"Look, Ms. Waters…"

"Toni," she corrected eagerly.

"… I've already accepted the position. I can't go back on my word."

"If your only worry is your integrity, I can handle that. I know some people and I can assure you, your name will be intact if you withdraw from the city's offer."

"My staying is that important to you?"

The restroom door pushed open and someone entered before Toni could answer.

"I think we need to take this conversation back to our table. Ladies…" Grand Waters walked past them and headed back to the table with both women in tow.

Kyle stood when Miranda approached him. "You ready to go?"

"Sit down, Kyle," Grand Waters ordered as her son helped her into her seat. "Miranda will have to learn how to deal with Toni and her outbursts. Better sooner than later if you plan to have her be a part of this family."

Kyle looked over at Miranda who had already sat in her seat, so he did the same.

"Now, I think it's time you all tell Miranda the real story of why you want her to stay."

"Kyle is the one that wanted to keep it a secret, not me," Toni tattled.

"That's only because I didn't want her to think I wanted to date her to keep her employed, Toni."

"Well, I say the truth is always better, little brother."

"You know what I think, it will be better for her to leave just so she doesn't have to deal with your arrogant behind."

"Enough!" Kyle's father's voice rumbled. He looked from his son to his daughter, and then directed his gaze on Miranda. "My adult children are acting like youngsters and it's ugly."

Miranda looked over at Kyle and smiled. She thought he looked cute when he was angry.

Mr. Waters continued. "It's like this, Miranda; the company will not sign unless you lead the project. So I think a bonus of two percent of the net profit should help persuade you to stay a part of KBW. You'll get the bonus after the project is completed, of course. I'll have that drawn up as a part of the deal."

Miranda's shook her head. "Mr. Waters, it's truly not about the money. The money is great, but I'm more worried about how my coworkers will view this whole thing. You see, I'm really fond of your son and I really would like this relationship to have a chance to develop into something special. I don't want my life to be a part of the office gossip."

"I see. I can handle that."

"How can you handle what people say?" Miranda asked incredulously.

"That's easy. I'll make a new rule. Anyone participating in office gossip will be fired immediately."

"You can't be serious." Miranda chuckled as she looked over at Grand Waters.

"He's serious, sweetie," she answered.

"I know I can't make you stay. I can only attempt to persuade you by using a salary increase, bonuses, and rule changes." He repositioned himself in his chair. "Now let me just say that my son flatly refused to try and influence you to stay in any way. Under normal circumstances Kyle would have been the one to make the offer. But he refused to even negotiate with you. Now that I've met you, I understand why." He smiled at Miranda. "I like you. I've been admiring your work for some time now. Chris thinks very highly of you and ever since you and Chris have been working together, I've seen a total turnaround in the company. Chris says you go above and beyond the call of duty and that you are honest, imaginative, and committed." Mr. Waters adjusted his tie. "But, I'm not about to beg. If you are the woman that my son thinks you are, now that you have the real story behind your importance of staying, I'm sure you'll make the right decision. Now, unless you have any questions, we are finished with this conversation so we can enjoy what's left of the evening." He paused to give Miranda room to speak.

She shook her head. "No."

"Are you sure?"

"I'm sure," she affirmed.

"Kyle asked that we not discuss business this evening and we broke that promise. We all owe him an apology." He looked over at his son. "I'm sorry for making a promise I didn't keep. But, I'm not sorry that all of this is in the open. Now, who would like dessert?"

Chapter Fourteen

After leaving the mountains, Sheena decided to go to her apartment rather than go back to her parents' house. They went to Ivy's house first since that's where Marshall had left his car. Then Marshall volunteered to take Sheena to pick up a few groceries and take her home. Ivy had been a little concerned about her being alone, but after talking with Sheena's parents, it was agreed that her decision to go home was a sign of progress.

Marshall helped Sheena put the food away and afterward he walked into her living room. He admired her taste in decorating and her DVD collection. That's when he noticed a photo of her and Jason resting on the entertainment center. He picked up the heavy silver-framed photo to examine it more closely. He knew it was silly, but he felt jealousy creep in as he gazed at the picture.

"I guess I need to put that photo away," she said, startling him.

"Well, it's a nice picture of you," he remarked with a smile.

Sheena smiled back at him. "I'm going to find a replacement for it."

Marshall turned the frame facedown. "This will do until you and I take one of us to switch it with."

Sheena sat down on the sofa and removed her shoes, letting out a soft moan. He moved to the sofa and sat next to her placing her feet in his lap and began massaging them.

She leaned her head back against the sofa and closed her eyes. "Hmm… that feels good."

"Your feet are sore, because you were on your feet longer than the horse was."

"Oh, I know I was on the horse, because my backside hurts too."

"You want me to rub that as well?" he joked.

"Ha, ha… you are really funny," Sheena gave a fake chuckle. She closed her eyes, relaxing completely.

"Don't forget about our dinner date tomorrow night," Marshall reminded her.

"I won't." She was falling asleep on him.

"Well, I guess I'll let you settle in for the night."

"Leaving me so soon?" she asked, yawning.

"Yeah, I'm going into the office for a few hours tomorrow."

"Oh, I thought you didn't have to be back until Wednesday."

"I don't, but I wanted to go over some files before the deposition on Wednesday afternoon, and you need to sleep." He placed her legs on the floor and stood.

"Oh, okay." She gave him a half-smile. "Thank you, Marshall. For everything you've done this week."

"No problem, no problem at all."

Sheena got up to walk him to the door. He turned to say, "If you need to talk, call me any time. I mean that."

"I know you do. And I appreciate your kindness." Sheena gave him a quick hug, stepped back, and opened the door for him.

"Tomorrow night?"

"I'll be ready."

He stepped outside her apartment. "Oh, one question?"

"Yes?"

"Do you still want me to see if my friend can schedule you for a consultation?"

"I don't know, Vincent. It seems talking with you has been good therapy."

"Then that's a no?"

"Let's just see what happens in the next few days."

He nodded his reply and she closed the door.

☙❧

Miranda needed to talk to her friends. She knew that Sheena was in a crisis, but so was she. Knowing that Ivy and Sheena were probably just now getting back in town, she dialed Jade's number.

"Hello." It was Jade's husband, Darrell.

"Hi, Darrell, is your wife around?"

"Yeah, can I get her to call you back? I'm on the line."

"Sure, thanks."

She stared at the phone after hanging up. "What should I do, Lord? Tell me what to do," she implored out loud.

She went to her mother's bedroom to check on her. She had fallen asleep while reading her Bible. Miranda removed the book from her mother's chest and the glasses from her eyes, placing them both on the nightstand.

Miranda had wanted to share her dilemma with her mother. But the new medication she was on kept her from being focused. She had called to complain to her mother's doctor about it, but he told her that the old medication was no longer effective and that this new prescription was the only thing that could keep her comfortable without her being hospitalized. Her mother had been adamant about not wanting to go back into the hospital, so she had to deal with it.

She kissed her mother's cheek. "Sleep tight, Mama." She turned off the light and closed the door. When the phone rang twenty minutes later she scooped it up immediately, "Hi, Jade."

"No, it's not, Jade."

"Oh, Kyle."

"Oh, wow, you sound disappointed."

"No, it's just that I was waiting for Jade to call me back."

"Well, I just called to see if you'd like to see a movie with me?"

"Not tonight, but thanks. My mother just started this new medication and I need to stay home so I can see how she's reacting to it."

"Then how about I bring a movie over to your house?"

"Hold on, let me get the other line. Hello?"

"Hey, Randi."

"Ivy, you're home?"

"Yeah, Jade's on the line too."

"Oh, I really need to talk to you guys. Hold on; let me get Kyle off the phone…. Kyle?"

"I'm still here."

"Let me call you back."

"Can I just head over there?"

"I'll call you back, stay put."

"All right, I'm put."

Miranda clicked back over to Jade and Ivy. "I need you all to help me make a decision."

"You're not talking about whether you should stay or leave KBW, are you?"

"Yes, Jade. I need to make the right choice here."

"Okay, you're going to have to get me up to speed on this," Ivy said.

Miranda gave Ivy and Jade the full story from the initial offer at the office on Monday to Kyle calling her and asking if he could bring over a movie that evening.

"Well, if I were you, I'd take the money," Jade said with a giggle. "I don't see what's so hard about it."

"You love the job," Ivy chimed in. "You like the people you work with and Ms. Toni just may end up being your sister-in-law, which means the money will still be in the family," Ivy finished with a snigger.

"Ha, ha, ha, I'm serious."

"I'm serious, too. I guarantee you that you mother will say the same thing. So what's your problem?" Ivy demanded.

"Keep the job you love, Randi. Don't leave just because you're in love with your boss!" Jade continued to find humor in Miranda's circumstances.

"But in all seriousness, you'll have to make this decision for yourself. It's you that will have to live with whatever option you go with. You asked us what we would do if we were in your position and both of us told you that we would stay. But we are not you," Ivy pointed out.

"Look, Randi, you're good at what you do, and you now know they know you're good at what you do, and they're willing to pay you for what you are worth to them. It's a blessing. Accept it," Jade said.

"Randi, even the Bible says come as a child. My children have never said, *no mommy, I don't want your gift.*"

"You are so right, Ivy. We got Desmond a new bike yesterday for no reason at all. He simply said, *thank you daddy, thank you mommy.*"

Miranda laughed, "I hear you, and I understand."

"Good," Ivy said.

"Now, moving on. I need you two to check on Sheena from time to time. She didn't go back to her parents' house."

"She went home?" Jade asked.

"Yes, so we need to keep an eye on her."

"Did she enjoy the trip?" Miranda asked.

"I think she did. We both ended up a little sore from horseback riding on our last day there, but other than that, we had a great time."

"Well, I can check on her each afternoon. KBW isn't far from her apartment."

"Yes!" Jade exclaimed. "You're going to stay!"

Miranda relented. "Yes, I told you I heard you."

"Good choice, Randi," Ivy applauded.

"Let me talk to you two later. I need to return Kyle's call."

"Good night!" both women shouted.

Miranda disconnected their call and pressed in Kyle's phone number. He answered on the first ring. "Can I leave now? I have the movie and some microwave popcorn."

Miranda laughed, "No, I have to work tomorrow."

"It's not late yet, it's only…. eight o'clock."

"Yes, I know and by the time you leave it will be midnight."

"Okay, my feelings are hurt. You just don't want to see me."

"Well, I'll see you tomorrow, won't I?"

"Dinner at six?"

"Hmm, what about lunch at one?"

"One?"

"One," Miranda confirmed.

"Where?"

"Buddakan on Chestnut Street?"

Kyle laughed. "You're joking right?"

"No, I love that place."

"Yes, I know you love that place, but if you go there on your first day of work, it just might be your last day of work."

"So, you would fire me if I'm more than an hour for lunch?"

Kyle was silent.

"Be at your Center City Office by twelve-thirty and don't be late. Goodnight, Kyle." She hung up the phone without hearing his reply.

Chapter Fifteen

It was Monday and Sheena had enjoyed being all alone for the first time since she was hospitalized. She woke early that morning, took a long bubble bath, and then sat in her kitchen to enjoy a simple bran muffin and a cup of hot tea.

She went through the pile of junk mail that had been accumulating for weeks. Not only had her parents changed her phone number, email address, and cell number for her protection, but they also took care of the important mail like her car insurance, rent, and utilities. So the only thing left for her to go through was the junk mail.

Before noon she had talked to her parents, then with Ivy early in the afternoon, and Miranda and Jade by late afternoon then with Marshall checking on her by evening. He was picking her up for dinner at Ava Restaurant. For months she had wanted to go there. Sheena loved Italian food and Marshall told her Ava had the best.

Sheena wanted to look nice for what she considered her first official date with Marshall. It took her more than a half hour to choose a dress. It was hard finding one that fit because she was thinner than usual and her clothing didn't fit like she wanted it to. Nevertheless, she finally decided on a Maggy London black silk halter dress. She'd purchased it over a year before and had never worn it. She removed the tags and slid it on her body. She smiled. It looked good. She pinned her hair up off her shoulders to create a more sophisticated look. She never wore makeup, but she powered her face to get rid of the shine, then she applied a peach-colored lip gloss to give her lips luster. Just when she was assessing herself in the mirror, the phone rang.

"Hello?"

"Good evening, Ms. Sheena. Welcome back home."

"Hello, Anthony. It's good to be back. I assume Mr. Marshall is here for me?"

"No, it's not Mr. Marshall. She says her name is Josephine Knight."

"Oh... okay..."

"Shall I let her up?"

"Yes... please.... and, Anthony?"

"Ma'am?"

"I'm expecting Vincent Marshall, will you let him up when he gets here."

"Yes, ma'am."

Sheena hung up the phone and went to her closet to select a pair of shoes. The four-inch ankle strap, black and gold stilettos that had been purchased with the dress she was wearing were perfect, so she chose them. By the time she slid on the shoes, Josephine rang the bell.

Sheena opened the door and greeted her with a smile. "Hi, Josephine, how are you?" She stepped aside for the other woman to enter.

Josephine hesitated as her lips parted slightly.

"You want to come in?" Sheena asked, confused.

"Um, yes.... thank you," Josephine finally answered as she followed Sheena into the living room. She turned to face Josephine, "can I offer you something to drink?"

"Um... no, thanks," she stammered. "I see you're probably on your way out..."

"Yes, I have a date."

"I see... wow... you've healed so nicely and you look stunning! I'm sure he'll be pleased."

Sheena innocently tilted her head to one side. "To God be the glory. But thank you, Josephine. So tell me, why are you here?"

"I wanted to be the first to tell you that the person who attacked you was arrested late last night."

Sheena's eyes widened with surprise. "That's great news. Why don't you have a seat?" She pointed to the chair opposite the love seat she'd just sat on. "How did they find him?"

"It wasn't a him, it's a woman."

Sheena sat up straight, clearly taken aback by the information. "A female attacked me?"

Josephine nodded.

"Are you sure?" she asked, still not believing her ears.

"Yeah, the photos I got from the bank camera gave us a good view of her once we had the film enhanced."

"Wow... a woman. I never thought.... I mean I never saw.... her coming."

Josephine moved to sit next to Sheena on the love seat and took both her hands in her own. "That's not the worst of it."

A moment of fear gripped her, "What?"

"I... um... I know her, Sheena."

There was a short pause while Sheena processed that bit of information. "You know her?"

"Yeah, she was a friend of mine up until about six months ago."

Sheena pulled her hands free from Josephine, never allowing her eyes to leave her face. "Has she admitted to attacking me?"

Josephine nodded. "Yes, but only after she was told about the surveillance cameras; and once she was shown the footage, she confessed."

Sheena's mind started racing. Josephine was talking, but she was still dealing with the fact that the person who had attacked her so brutally had been a female and a friend of her co-worker.

"...and she was formally arrested and charged with attempted murder. No one wants a trial and she's..."

"Did she say why she attacked me?" Sheena interrupted her mid-sentence.

"In her confession, she stated that she did it because she had lost me to you."

Sheena stood up abruptly. "But, there never was a *me and you*!" Sheena almost shouted.

"Yes, you and I know that, but a person who is delusional can't separate fact from fiction."

"Delusional?"

Josephine nodded. "She has some mental issues. I'm sure of it now."

"And you and this woman.... you were lovers?"

"Yes. But I swear to you, Sheena. I never imagined she'd go this far." Josephine sighed. "She was really jealous. That's why we separated in the first place. Even after we broke up, she continued to accuse me of being unfaithful to her."

"I don't believe this."

"I thought they were idle threats. She'd threatened before to kill anyone I saw and nothing ever happened, so I just thought it was another empty threat."

"I don't believe this," Sheena repeated in dismay.

"I didn't know she was following me around and snooping out my friends."

There was a knock at the door and Sheena knew it was Marshall. "Come in, it's open," she yelled as she moved to lean against the chair closest to the door. "So, she attacked me thinking I was involved with you romantically?"

Josephine started toward the door while buttoning her jacket, "that's what she said."

Sheena's back was toward Marshall when he entered the room, "Our reservation is at six, we need to get a….." he stopped after noticing they were not alone. "Hello," he greeted Josephine.

"Hi," Josephine answered. "Well, we can talk about this another time."

"No, we can talk about this now."

"I thought maybe you'd want to talk privately and besides, you're on your way…"

"No, you can finish telling me everything right here and now. I have nothing to hide from Marshall."

Marshall could see Sheena was clearly upset, especially since she'd converted back to calling him by his last name. "What's going on?"

Sheena turned to face him. "It was a woman who attacked me. She and Josephine were lovers."

"Josephine?"

"Yes, this is Josephine. Josephine Knight. I told you about her, remember?"

He nodded. "Yes, I remember."

"It seems I was caught in a love triangle I didn't know I was a part of." Sheena wanted to cry, but she was too angry to do so.

Marshall moved closer to her with outstretched arms and she stepped into his embrace.

"Sheena, I'm really sorry. The District Attorney's Office will be contacting you. They'll give you any other details you want."

Sheena pressed her cheek to Marshall's chest. He nodded to Josephine.

"I'll let myself out."

They listened as she headed to the door, opened it, and gently closed it behind her.

Marshall and Sheena stood right there with him holding her in his embrace while stroking her back in a comforting motion with no words passing between them.

After a full minute, Sheena pulled away. She was still fuming, and even though she knew Josephine couldn't control another person's actions, she was still annoyed about the whole situation.

"Are you all right?" Marshall asked concerned.

"Yes… No….. Yes, I'm so sorry. I was all ready to leave when she came here."

"Well, you look absolutely beautiful. We're going to Ava's and then we're going to the symphony."

She shook her head. "I can't go now, Marshall."

That was the second time she had called him Marshall and not Vincent. "What's my name?"

She turned to him and gave a sad smile, "I'm sorry, Vincent. But, I'm not up to going now."

He pulled her back into his arms and gave her a tight hug. "Don't worry, I'll get you in the mood," he said and then stepped away from her. "Where is your wrap?"

"Vincent…"

"Where is your wrap?" he asked again.

"It's lying across my bed."

Marshall walked past her and came back with her shawl. He draped it around her shoulders and then turned her to face him. "You lost most of your lipstick on my jacket."

She smiled up at him. "I don't wear lipstick. It's lip gloss."

"Then, go put the shine back on your lips so we can leave."

She took in a deep breath and blew it out slowly in an effort to calm herself. "I don't know if I'm going to be able to relax after this."

"Sheena," he called her name softly and she looked over at him. "We're going out as planned and we're going to have a wonderful time. Okay?"

She looked at him silently.

He took her hand and kissed her palm. "Trust me."

༄༅

It was almost 12:00 midnight when Sheena and Marshall returned from their first real date. Marshall counted it as a success even though she had called him Jason twice. The food at Ava Restaurant had been scrumptious and the Symphony was outstanding. On the drive to her apartment, Sheena kissed Marshall's cheek and told him she was glad he'd urged her to go despite the fact that Josephine's visit had upset her so much.

Marshall was sitting in the living room waiting for her to change her clothes. He had removed his tie and suit jacket. Now he was looking through her CDs, making a mental note of her taste in music.

Sheena was irritated with herself. While sitting in the restaurant, she had called him Jason. She had asked him to forgive her and he seemed to accept her apology with understanding by telling her not to worry about it. Still, she was beating herself up for the mishap. "If you want something to drink, I have juice and flavored water in the frig," Sheena yelled to Marshall. She was standing in her closet wondering what to change into.

"Can I play some music?" he hollered back as he held a disk in his hand labeled Stevie Wonder that she had apparently downloaded from the internet.

"Sure," she answered as she continued to scan her closet for the right thing to change into. "What is wrong with me? It's just Marshall," she reasoned with herself. "So why am I so nervous?" She paused a moment realizing she knew why. She and Marshall weren't just friends. They had been on a real date and she had enjoyed every moment of it.

She decided to slip on a pair jeans and a t-shirt and just as she exited her bedroom, she heard Stevie singing *A Ribbon In The Sky*, one of her favorite songs. When she reached the living room, Marshall turned to her and held out his hand. Sheena went to him with a smile, took his hand, and he pulled her into his arms. As they began to slowly sway to the music, Sheena gazed into his eyes. She had never been a dancer, but with guidance from Marshall, she was able to sync to the rhythm as if she'd been dancing for years.

Sheena liked being close to him and because she trusted him she was able to relax, totally. She pressed her face to his chest enjoying the hardness of his body, the smell of his cologne, the touch of his hand, and the very beat of his heart.

And for that very moment, everything was just how it should be - perfect.

Chapter Sixteen

Sheena had been dating Vincent Marshall for almost two months when Ivy called her and asked if they could have a girl's night out at her apartment instead of having it at a restaurant. Sheena agreed and told Ivy to bring dessert, Miranda to bring some sparkling apple cider, and for Jade to bring her Family Feud DVD game for entertainment and she would cook.

Ivy and Miranda were the first to arrive at Sheena's house. The smell of the food met them at the elevator.

"All I want to know is, where's the chef?" Miranda asked, "'cause I know Sheena didn't prepare food, so it had to be catered." She handed Sheena a large bag and she knew from the sound that it was a few bottles of sparkling apple cider inside.

"Yes, I did," Sheena laughed at Miranda's comment as she let them in, leading them to the kitchen. "You brought your Bible, Randi?"

"Just like Visa, I don't leave home without it."

"Seriously though, Sheen, where did you buy the food, it smells yummy," Miranda said as she looked towards the noise of the chime.

"Get the door, you know that's Jade," Sheena said looking at Miranda.

"If you didn't hire a chef, then you must have asked a neighbor to help," Miranda accused her playfully as she left to answer the door.

"I'm telling you the truth. I made everything on my own, and I do mean everything on this table," she yelled to her back.

"Yeah, yeah."

"You probably need to tell them about those cooking classes," Ivy whispered.

"No way."

"Okay."

"Hey, everybody," Jade gave each woman a hug.

"Why didn't you meet us so we could ride together?" Ivy asked.

"One of my students came to me in confidence, asking me questions about homosexuality. So I had to take the time and talk with him. I pulled out a few scriptures and when I got to the one in 1st Corinthian 6:9-10, he asked me what was an *effeminate.*"

"I don't even know what that is," Ivy said.

"An effeminate is a man who appears to have unsuitable feminine qualities."

"Wow, I didn't know your very appearance could be unsuitable," Ivy remarked.

"Well, part of that scripture says, nor abusers of themselves with mankind will inherit the kingdom of heaven and once I said that, he raised his head and asked me, does this mean I won't go to heaven? I simply told him to read the Word for himself, because the bible says what it means, and means all that it say. I certainly didn't write the book."

"It must be an epidemic especially among the youth," Miranda commented.

"That's who Satan is after, the innocent ones," Ivy said.

"Well, I told him I had a friend that I wanted him to talk to," Jade looked at Sheena.

"Who me?"

"Yes, you."

"Oh, no. I can't talk to anyone about their sexuality. You need to tell him to talk to a professional, and I'm no good in that area."

"You can talk to the boy, Sheena. He's only..."

"No, Jade. I'm not talking to anyone about homosexuality."

"I'm not asking you to…"

"End of conversation."

"But…"

"That's final."

"Let it go, Jade," Ivy spoke softly.

"Check out the spread Sheena prepared for us," Miranda said changing the subject.

The women were staring at the spread of food on the table. Ivy had already sampled Sheena's new cooking skills while they were on their mountain retreat and she knew about the cooking classes, but she promised to keep that knowledge a secret.

"Wow, not only has she learned to dance, but she's learned to cook too," Jade said in astonishment.

"Well, all I have to say is Marshall must be a miracle worker," Miranda joked.

"Ha, ha, ha … you are real funny, Ms. Thing."

"What, the man has pulled you out of the funk you were in…" Miranda continued.

"Gave you rhythm…" Ivy added.

"Got you cooking…" Jade put in her two cents worth as she pulled out a chair to sit at the table.

"She has a little influence on him too," Ivy said.

"How is that?" Jade asked.

"Marshall's been attending church regularly, haven't you all noticed?"

"I have," Miranda agreed.

"Oh, no she didn't, look Ivy, Randi, this heifer has cooked homemade lasagna!" Jade was amazed.

"Oh, yeah, he's getting her ready for the march," Miranda added matter-of-factly, sitting down as well.

"The march?" Both Ivy and Jade asked almost in unison.

"Da da da-da..." Miranda started humming the wedding march.

"Oh, so that's his plan!" Ivy threw back her head and hooted. Jade and Miranda joined in.

"Oh, like the march only pertains to me, please." Sheena turned to Ivy. "Did you tell them your latest news, Ms. Know-It-All?"

Ivy stopped laughing. "Not now, Sheena."

"What? You didn't tell them?" Sheena asked accusingly.

"Tell us what?" Miranda asked.

"Well, you all wanted to know why I had Ivy's children over the weekend..."

"Yeah," Miranda said.

"Well, that's because Bill wanted time with Ivy alone so he could..." Sheena paused, as she watched Ivy cast a deadly look her way. "Do you want to tell them or would you like me to continue?" Sheena asked, looking directly at Ivy.

Ivy lifted her head. "Bill and I are getting married!" she blurted out.

The room went completely silent. Sheena looked over at Miranda, then Jade, who both looked stunned. "Well, it's about time," Jade finally cried out as she made her way to Ivy to embrace her.

"Wow, I'm jealous." Miranda said. "But I'm happy for you, girl." Miranda made her way to her cousin giving her a kiss on the cheek.

"So tell us how he proposed," Jade wanted to know.

"Yeah, and don't leave out one detail," Miranda said.

"Well, Bill had taken the kids out Saturday morning and I'd been worried about him spending so much time with us. I felt like we were just too involved in his life and I'd planned on telling him so when he dropped the kids off. Anyway, when he brought the kids home, he was acting strange. I knew something was up 'cause even the kids were acting funny."

"He had the kids in on it too?" Miranda asked.

Ivy nodded. "I knew something was up, even though I had no earthly idea it would be a marriage proposal." Ivy paused and the women could tell she was remembering the event because a wide smile creased her face.

"Now you know we want all the details, so don't leave out nothing," Miranda rested her elbows on the table to relax her head against her hand.

"Details, okay, well, it went like this..."

Bill sat down and Ivy stared at him from across the kitchen table. After a few moments Bill asked, "What?"

"That's what I want to know," Ivy answered.

He shrugged. "I haven't the slightest idea what you're talking about."

"You're up to something, Bill Hart."

Ignoring her statement, he asked, "Did you finish your garden masterpiece?"

Ivy's eyes lit up with delight. "Yes!" She jumped up and headed to the back door. "Come on, let me show you!"

"I'll look at it later, okay? Because..."

"No!" Ivy cried and moved to where he was sitting. Grabbing his hand, she pulled him up. "Come on, Bill. I'm so proud of myself," she said, holding his hand and leading him through the door and out into the garden.

"Wow, it's beautiful!" Bill said in amazement.

"Yeah, man. And you said I couldn't do it."

"No, I never said you couldn't do it. I said it was a lot of work and you'd probably need some help."

"But I didn't need any help! And look, the fountain is working perfectly," Ivy said.

"Yes, it is. Wow, I can't believe you did all this!" He was smiling proudly.

She turned to him, suddenly serious. "Bill, I need to talk to you."

"Yeah, about what?"

"About the kids and me... well... we've been monopolizing your time."

Bill shot her a look. "Have I complained?"

"No. But you should. Just a few weeks ago you were talking about how much you'd like to get married and have a family. But, you're spending so much time with us that you don't have time to have a life of your own."

"I think there's a lot of things you don't know about me," he said gently. "For one, I don't hang out in places I don't want to be. Two, I love those kids in there"– he pointed to the house – "and three, I love you, Ivy."

Ivy smiled. "I love you too, Bill. But you need romance and I do, too. Actually, we're blocking each other."

"Oh, so that's what this is about," Bill said. "It's not about me, it's about you."

"Bill."

"Oh, no, I get it. You want to date and I'm in the way. I see."

"No that's not what I mean at all. You're twisting what I'm trying to say. Just let me explain."

He frowned. "Okay, go ahead."

"I just think that we hog all your free time and we're getting too attached to you. You're here on Saturdays and all day Sunday. Last week you took the boys fishing, and today, on your day off, you took the kids to the amusement park."

"I do it..."

Ivy put her finger over his lips to stop him. "It's not just the kids Bill... it's me."

"Mom, Aunt Sheena is here," Ray Junior called from the house.

The moment seemed lost, and they both left the gazebo quietly, each pursuing individual thoughts. When they got to the house, Sheena came over to Bill and whispered something to him. "Thanks, Sheena," Bill said as he pushed something into his pants pocket.

Sheena asked Ivy's children, "You guys all ready?"

The children hollered, "Yeah."

"Good, so say goodbye to Bill and your mother. We need to put a move on, 'cause we don't want to be late."

"Late for what?" Ivy asked at last, puzzled.

"Bill, you haven't talked to her!"

"I didn't get a chance."

"Well, you'll have the chance in a moment, 'cause we're out of here," Sheena said.

"Wait a minute. Where you goin' with my children?"

"Don't worry about where I'm going. You worry about where you're going since you don't have to worry about your crumb snatchers until tomorrow night," Sheena answered.

"Yeah, Mom. Have fun for once," Ray Junior said and then walked over to his mother and kissed her cheek. "Make sure she has lots of fun, okay?" he asked Bill.

Bill put a fist to his chest. "You know I will." Ray Junior smiled.

Ivy watched as Sheena took her children, leaving her and Bill alone. After Bill closed the door behind Sheena, he leaned against it and fixed his eyes on Ivy.

Ivy turned and walked into the kitchen and sat in the seat she had vacated earlier. Picking up her glass of cider, she sipped it slowly, "what's going on, Bill?"

"Let's finish the conversation we had just before Sheena came," he said and sat next to her at the table.

"I don't want to talk about that anymore."

"Well, I do. Let me see where we left off. You said that you and the kids hog all my time."

"Well it's true and..."

Bill put his finger over her lips. "It's my turn to speak."

"But..."

"And then you said... let me see if I can remember correctly... you said, it's not just the kids, it's me."

Ivy stood up. "I'm not going to be interrogated by you."

"I'm not trying to interrogate you, baby."

Ivy looked at him. He called me baby, *she murmured to herself.*

"I'm just telling you what I told you earlier," Bill continued. "I love you, Ivy."

"I love you too, but..."

"No, you don't understand. I'm in love with you, baby. I don't want to be with anybody else. I don't want to date anybody else, and I don't want you seeing anybody else. I... love... you."

"You're in love with me?"

"Yes, I'm in love with you. I know you care for me 'cause you and I really click, girl." Bill moved directly in front of her and dropped to one knee.

Ivy placed her hands over her breast, "I gasped for air 'cause I couldn't breathe. He reached in his pocket and pulled out this." She held her left hand up and for the first time the girls noticed the huge diamond on her finger. "Then he asked, will you marry me?"

"Oh, Ivy! That's so beautiful. Check out that ring." Miranda was teary-eyed as she examined it.

"Oh, it's beautiful, Ivy. Now I know why you have that gleam on your face!" Jade said.

Miranda placed her hands together in prayer and looked toward the ceiling. "Dear Lord, within a year or so, please direct Kyle to do something similar."

All the girls laughed.

"Well, anyway, we have a wedding to plan," Miranda said.

"No we don't." Ivy corrected her immediately.

"What do you mean, no?" Miranda gasped. "You already got married?"

"No. We're going to do it at my house. No big, medium, or small wedding; and I mean that." Ivy looked at each of her friends one by one. "Am I making myself clear?"

"Why?" Miranda asked.

"Yeah, Ivy, we want to be a part of it." Sheena complained.

"Look, I already had a big wedding the first time and so did Bill. So we want to keep it simple. But you all can be there. You know I wouldn't get married without my girls being there. So with you, my parents, my brother and his wife, and Bill's immediate family, I say about twenty-five people will be the maximum. So I'm telling you, if you try doing anything different, we will elope, and this I promise you."

"Well, okay," Miranda said after taking a sip of apple cider. "So, when are you going to do this simple ceremony?"

"Two weeks from now."

"Two weeks?" Miranda gasped and choked immediately.

"Girl, I feel you. Been there and had to do that quick thing." Jade nodded her understanding. She and her husband Darrell had married quickly only a few short months before. "It's better to marry than to burn in desire." Jade and Ivy burst into laughter.

Miranda and Sheena looked at each other and shook their heads.

Sheena poured herself some cider and looked over at her friends. "Vincent gave me this a few days ago." She handed a white envelope to Jade. She opened it immediately and the room was quiet as she scanned the two-page document.

"What is it?" Miranda was curious.

After a few more minutes, Jade looked at Sheena, "Is he serious?"

"Very."

"Well what is it?" Ivy asked as she took the document from Jade's hand.

"It's a marriage proposal from Marshall," Jade finally answered.

"What?" Ivy was agape as she scanned the papers.

"We talked about a marriage partnership a few times. But most of the time it was in passing or simply joking around. I never imagined he would draw up a contract and ask me to consider it."

"So, you're taking this into consideration?" Jade was completely astonished.

"Yes."

"Do you love him?" Miranda asked.

"No."

"Then there's nothing to consider," Miranda said with finality.

"Why do I have to be in love with him before I marry him?" Sheena asked seriously.

"Sheen, sweetie… It's hard enough living with a man you love, but without the love, where will that leave you? Love is what covers faults, sweetie. When you get upset with him, it's love that makes you hold on for better or for worse, in sickness and in health, and it's love that drives a couple to stick and stay." Ivy's voice was sensible.

"Look, it won't be long before I'm thirty-five, then forty. I want children and I'm tired of being alone. I don't see anything wrong with making a decision with my mind. Just about all the other choices we make, like what we do for a living or where we live or what car we purchase, are all done with our minds not our hearts. I trust my mind, but not my heart."

The room was silent as each woman stared at her.

Sheena pressed on, since everybody was shocked. "Jade everyone is not as fortunate as you to come here from the south and meet a man like Darrell, fall in love and end up happily married." Then she turned to Miranda. "And you can't stop talking about Kyle! You haven't known him that long, and you already know that you want to marry him."

Miranda grinned widely.

"And tell me who is more blessed than Ivy to have found love not once, but twice."

Jade shook her head. "Sheen, I told you about Preston Owens. I told you how he confessed to me that he married a woman he didn't love, and now look at him. Ten years and two kids later, they're in the middle of a divorce and look who suffers, the children."

"This is different, Jade." Sheena paused, taking a deep breath, "Preston Owens went into that relationship lying about his feelings. Vincent and I know we're not in love. We know this is a partnership for the reasons outlined in that agreement," she said as she pointed to the papers in Ivy's hand. "Look, I won't be the only one in this world who got married this way. As a matter of fact, marriages of convenience have a tendency to last when traditional marriages fail."

"All I know is, less than two months ago, you were in a deep depression over Jason, who we all know is your one true love. So I can't see you ever being able to be committed to a loveless marriage, not when I know how you feel about Jason," Ivy argued.

"Look, we'll have the agreement and that's what we'll be committed to."

"Committed to a man-made document? Well, I don't like it one bit. I think you're out of your damn' mind to even consider marrying a man you don't love," Jade said, shocking everyone.

Miranda leaned back in her chair and poured herself another glass of apple cider, waiting for Jade and Sheena to exchange verbal blows. It wasn't too many times they could get together and not debate about something.

"Look, I know I'm the last one to be giving advice 'cause I jacked up my own life with my own bad advice, but I'm telling you Sheen, you've been too confused about too much stuff to make a decision of this magnitude."

"So what are you saying, Jade?" Sheena took offense.

"What I'm saying is that this isn't something to just take lightly, Sheena. Just a few short months ago you said you'd never get married."

"No, I said I probably would never get married."

"Just a few months ago you and that woman what's her name?"

"Josephine," Miranda supplied just before taking a sip of apple cider.

"Yeah, Josephine was hanging together and…"

"She was a bowling partner, that's it. You know it and I know it, but most of all God knows it."

"Well, her girlfriend didn't know it."

"That's enough," Ivy warned loudly, giving Jade a sharp look. "You two will not argue today."

Jade bowed her head in submission. Then Ivy turned to Sheena whose eyes were fixed on Jade. "I don't even know why I shared this with any of you."

"You really just mean me, don't you?" Jade asked argumentatively.

"I said I'm not having it, so shut up, both of you," Ivy reiterated between clinched teeth before Sheena could answer Jade.

"Look, let's all just eat and talk about this rationally," Miranda said. "Sheena's cooked a wonderful meal and we're letting it get cold."

Sheena defiantly turned her gaze on Miranda.

"Come on, sit down. Ivy. Sheena, please just sit down," Miranda pleaded while filling a bowl with salad.

Ivy walked around the table to sit across from Miranda, "Let's pray so we can eat."

"I've always looked up to you, Sheen," Jade said just above a whisper. "I wanted to be just like you. That's why I followed you into law school. I saw in you what I wanted to be. You were able to remain virtuous no matter how many men were attracted to you. Even Jason was unable to make you drop your standards. I tried that with Darrell and I failed."

Sheena was amazed to hear that Jade reverenced her so highly. "Why would you put me so high on a pedestal when I'm just like you, I'm human. I'm not perfect."

"I know that, but you," Jade looked around the room at the other women, "all of you, have always aimed for perfection. After Ivy got married, I looked towards you more. I know that we are influenced by who we attached ourselves to, that's why I hung around you. I wanted you to rub off on me and you did. I wouldn't have thought about going to law school if it weren't for you. Do you remember my freshman year of college and you told me not to hang around the Andrews twins?"

Sheena nodded her head.

"You came to me in the library with your bible and told me to read 2nd Corinthians 6:17 which I learned by heart and it says, *Wherefore come out from among them, and be ye separate, saith the Lord, and touch not the unclean thing; and I will receive you.* And when you walked away from me you said and I quote, if you waddled with dogs, you'll get up with flees, unquote. I didn't want you to be influenced by that woman's thinking.

"Why wouldn't you think I would rub off on her instead of her rubbing off on me?" Sheena questioned.

"In your weakened state, I knew you were defenseless. You were hurting and trying your best to hide it. I've been in that state before. I saw the signs. I knew if she had the chance she'd confuse you more than you already were."

Sheena cast her eyes to the floor and said almost in a whisper, "I'm sorry I've disappointed you. But you know to keep your eyes on the Lord." Sheena raised her head to meet Jade's gaze. "Never allow man to order your steps. If I hadn't consulted the Word of God, I'd really be messed up right now. The Word is a lamp unto my feet and a light unto my pathway."

Jade smiled. "And I should know that better than anyone here. So I know there's no need for any of us to worry about you because God's got your back."

Sheena nodded. She had never looked at it that way. "All the way to my grave," she remark.

Ivy stood up. "You know, everything we've been through has been a test. God takes us to higher levels in him through those tests. Sheena's in the middle of a test and weapons have been formed against her, but my Bible says, they will not prosper."

"Amen," Miranda murmured.

"You have to go through this dilemma, to get to the other side, Sheena. So you do what you have to do, even if we don't understand it. Nobody can take my tests but me, so if I pass or fail, I can't blame anyone but me," Ivy said. "Take your test. You've been equipped with the Word Map."

"The Word Map?" Miranda was perplexed.

"Yes, the Word Map," Ivy confirmed. "The Word Map can get you out of any situation, no matter what it is."

"Oh, I get it." Miranda reached into her bag and pulled out her Bible. "The Word Map."

"You follow that map and you'll never go down the wrong road. And I know the Word Map will get you where you need to go and it will get you there safe."

"I know that's right," Jade agreed.

"What we need to do is stay in prayer for each other," Miranda added, "because it seems each of us is either just coming out of a test, or entering into one, or in the heart of one. But no matter where we are, we need each other. We're not just friends, we're family, and right now I think we need a group hug," Miranda stood and Ivy came to join her, then Sheena, and finally Jade. They hugged collectively and individually. Jade apologized to Sheena and all was forgiven.

Miranda sat down at the table first and demanded, "*Now*, can we eat?"

"Let's sit down and pray over this food," Ivy said, taking her seat.

"We'll need an extra strong prayer since Sheena's the one who cooked," Miranda said and giggled.

The other women joined in her laughter. Sheena shook her head quietly, knowing that those cooking classes had taught her well.

It was around eight when Sheena took the elevator to see her friends out.

"I still can't believe how good the food was," Miranda commented for the third time after she gave Sheena a hug and headed toward the exit.

"It was good Sheen. I'm proud of you girl," Jade said as she hugged Sheena goodbye. "Next month, we'll do girl's night out at my house. Oh and don't forget, the revival is next week. We promised Mother Evans that we'd support it.

"I plan to make a few nights," Sheena replied.

"Uncle James said the woman is a Prophet, so I'm really looking forward to it," Miranda added. "Good night Anthony."

"Good night ladies," Anthony said as he opened the door for the women.

Sheena had pushed the button to her floor when Anthony called to her.

"Ms. Sheena, I have something here for you." He pulled out a letter size envelope from his desk drawer. Sheena stood at the elevator holding the door opened as Anthony walked over to her. "Mr. Jackson gave it to me a few weeks ago. I had meant to give it to you, but I went on vacation for two weeks and had forgotten I put it in the drawer."

Sheena flipped the envelope reading her name and recognizing Jason's handwriting.

"I'm really sorry about this."

Sheena stepped on the elevator, "Thanks, Anthony."

Sheena went directly to her bedroom, sat on her bed, and read the letter.

Sheena:

I know you are upset with me and you have every right to be. As you probably already know, Ivy called me on the day you were admitted into the hospital. At the time she called, I was still angry with you and I never allowed Ivy to tell me anything. The day you were discharged from the hospital is the day I found out what happened to you. I've been trying to see you, but my efforts have been hindered in one way or another, so this will be my last attempt to contact you. Please call me. My cell number is still the same. I'll be here until Sunday, and if I don't hear from you, I'll know it's truly over between us.

Please know that if we never speak again that I still love you and know that I always will.

With all my heart,
Jason

Chapter Seventeen

The next morning, Sheena sat across from Vincent at a table at the Highway Diner watching him read the note Jason had left her.

"Looks like he wrote it while in the lobby of your apartment," he analyzed.

"I would assume so since it's written on the management stationary."

"So, did you call him?" Marshall asked.

Sheena nodded her head, "Yes, but I didn't talk to him. His voice message center was full."

Disappointment clouded his face. "It's my guess that this note has only uncovered feelings you've tried to bury."

Sheena dropped her head and blew out a sigh. "I tossed and turned all night long," she admitted. "When I got up this morning, I searched the internet for a round trip ticket from Philadelphia to Atlanta."

"So you booked a flight?"

She nodded. "Then, I called my mother and father and told them that I was going."

"She couldn't have been happy to hear that," he said matter-of-factly.

"No, she wasn't. My mother tried to talk me out of it."

"Are you going alone?" He seemed concerned.

She reached her arms across the table and grasped his hand in a comforting fashion. "Yes, I'm going alone, but I'll be fine," she assured him.

"Are you sure? I mean you haven't talked to him in months."

"I know, but it's important to me that I talk with him."

Marshall leaned back in his chair pulling his hand away from hers, "Well, I guess you have to do what you feel you need to do."

"Yes, I do. So, please don't be upset with me."

"Look, I like Jason. But his values aren't like ours. The two of you were brought up with a different standard of morals and I don't know if it can or will work out between the two of you."

"We were friends, Vincent. And maybe friendship is all we'll ever have, but right now, we're not even that. So it's important to me that we resolve our issues, because I love him and I don't want us to be estranged like we have."

"Then by all means go to him," Marshall threw up his hands in frustration.

"You're angry."

He answered her comment by shaking his head. "You haven't talked to him so he doesn't know you're coming?"

"I left him two messages, one at his office and the other at his house."

"Suppose he's out of town?"

"Then I probably won't see him and nothing will be resolved."

"You couldn't get one of the girls to go with you?" He stretched his arm across the table to give her back the note. "I'm sure Ivy wouldn't mind."

"No, I need to do this alone. Besides, I haven't told anyone other than you and my parents."

"Atlanta is a huge place," he countered.

"I'm from Camden, New Jersey - please!"

After meeting Marshall for breakfast, Sheena went home and packed. She decided to take a taxi to the airport. After being attacked, she still was not up to driving herself and leaving her car in a public garage. Everything was set, hotel and plane reservations. If need be, she would rent a car at the airport since her flight was scheduled to touch down in Atlanta at 9:09 PM. If she had not heard from Jason by then, she would go straight to the hotel and try reaching him again in the morning.

Just when she was about to call for a taxi the phone rang, "Hello."

"Hey, what time is your flight?"

She smiled, it was Marshall. "Seven."

"How are you getting to the airport?"

"Taxi, I was about to give them a call."

"Look, I'm not far from you, I can take you."

"Oh, no, I wouldn't think of asking you to do that."

"You didn't ask."

"Are you sure you want to…."

He interrupted her, "I'll see you in a few minutes."

In twenty minutes flat, Marshall was standing at Sheena's door.

"You don't have to do this."

"I know, but I just don't want you to think I'm upset with you.

Sheena smiled, "Oh really?"

"Yeah, I'm doing some major sucking up right now. Can't you see I've swallowed my pride?"

She smiled at him, "If you say so."

"Am I raking up any brownie points?"

"Oh, major points."

"Good." Marshall had intended to ask her if she'd thought anymore about his proposal. But it was clear, he wasn't on her mind. "This is all you have?" He asked pointing to the small piece of luggage by the door.

"That's it."

Marshall picked up the bag and headed for the elevator. Sheena locked her door and followed him. "I know you don't understand why I'm going?"

"I think I know why, and let's just leave it at that."

Marshall didn't want to hear her say again that she loved Jason. Not when he wanted her to love him more.

ಬಿಛ

Sheena arrived at Jason's front door at ten forty-five that night. She asked the taxi driver to wait because she knew he probably was not home since she didn't see a car in the driveway. She hadn't heard from him and when she tried to call his cell phone, she was still unable to leave a message, because the box was still full. Maybe Vincent was right she thought. He could be out of town, maybe even in Philadelphia. She was getting ready to leave a note in his mailbox when a car pulled into the driveway. When she turned, the lights blinded her vision, but they were quickly turned off.

Jason stepped from the vehicle. "Sheena?" He said with disbelief.

"Hi, I…, was leaving you.., a note," she stammered.

A wide smile creased his golden brown face as he rushed to her, scooping her up into his arms crushing her to his chest. There was no doubt that he was happy to see her. "I can't believe you're here. Damn, you look good. I've missed you," he murmured in her ear as he held her tight.

Sheena wrapped her arms around his neck. He still made her heart skip beats, why should she care that he's a Muslim. Sheena pulled back just enough to look up into his face, "I've missed you too."

"Do you mind? I have other fairs to get," the taxi driver said as he approached them.

"I need to take care of him," Sheena said softly.

"I'll handle it." Jason walked toward the driver as he reached in his back pocket for his wallet.

"So, you are the infamous Sheena Daniels."

Sheena swung her head toward the car Jason just pulled up in and for the first time she noticed he had a passenger. She wasn't surprised. Jason was always involved with at least one woman. However, of all the years she had known him, he had never been committed to anyone. He had always called his relationships maintenance dates, and he had been in Atlanta long enough to have a few of them by now.

The woman walked toward Sheena with an outstretched hand. "I'm Brenda Long."

Sheena greeted her by loosely grasping her hand, "Nice to meet you."

Brenda stared with a look of astonishment not letting go of her hand. Sheena forcibly pulled her hand from the woman's grasp.

"I'm sorry... I... He didn't lie... She stuttered. You're beautiful. Wow!" Her mouth was agape.

Jason was now coming toward them with Sheena's bag in hand, "Good you've made your own introductions."

Sheena dropped her gaze from the woman to look at Jason. "I'm intruding."

Jason shook his head and gestured using his hands to signal his disagreement.

"You shouldn't have let my taxi go." She reached in her purse for her cell phone. "I'll just call another and be out of your way."

"No. Nonsense," Jason finally declared taking the phone from her hand. "Let me get you into the house and then I'm going to take Brenda home."

Brenda's eyes sprang up giving Jason a direct stare with a frown on her face, "home?"

"Yes, I'm taking you home."

Sheena knew Jason's remark did not sit well with the woman. She was standing there in total trepidation.

"Get in the car," he directed to Brenda. "Sheena, you come with me," he said starting to the front door.

She had indeed put a wrench in their plans and she knew that was not fair to his friend. "Jason, I'll check into the. I already have reservations and we can …."

Jason gently gasped her hand moved her to the opened door. "Go into the house, Sheena," he motioned with his hands. "I don't have to tell you to make yourself at home. I'll be back shortly."

Sheena's glance went from Jason to Brenda, who was still standing in the driveway pouting, then back to Jason. "Are you sure? This doesn't feel right."

Jason dismissed her concern, "she lives about thirty minutes away so I shouldn't be too long."

Her gaze went back to the driveway. Brenda's intent look at her was fierce.

"I don't know. She seems pretty upset right now," Sheena said softy not taking her eyes from where Brenda was standing.

"Look at me," Jason ordered and she did. "I'm taking her home so you and I can talk. That's what you came for right?"

"Yes."

"Okay. Go in the house."

Sheena then stepped through the door into the living room.

"Wait for me in the car. I won't be long. I just want to get her settled," Jason said to Brenda.

Brenda called his name.

"Get in the car, please," he almost yelled then came into the house.

Sheena turned to him. "I assumed you didn't get any of my messages?"

"No, I had no idea you were coming."

"You shouldn't change your plans with your girlfriend just because I showed up."

"Right now I'm so glad to see you, I'm willing to change Gods."

Sheena was speechless.

He walked past her. Follow me. "There's two bedrooms, but only one has a bed," he walked towards the rear of the apartment and opened the last door at the end of the hall. "Make yourself comfortable."

"Jason, I don't think your girlfriend appreciates…"

"Don't worry about her. We'll talk when I get back."

ಬಿಂಗ

When Jason arrived home, Sheena was sleeping at the foot of his bed. He debated if he should wake her or not. Her hair fanned the pillow and one leg crossed the other making the number four. He had seen her like this many times before. Especially, when they would get on her bed and play an intense game of scrabble. He couldn't count how many times they had fallen asleep on her bed with him waking first and finding her just this way.

He wanted to know what made her come to him. But, he figured morning was only a few hours away and it could wait until then.

Jason took off his clothes and slipped on some pajama bottoms and a t-shirt. He stretched out on the bed facing her and her eyes bounced open.

She smiled at him and he smiled back. "I'm sorry. I fell asleep on you," she murmured.

"No problem. We'll talk in the morning."

She smiled once again and closed her eyes.

If this had been any other woman, he would have pulled her under him and had her panting in passion right now. Yet, he was content with just watching her sleep.

ಬಲ

Morning had arrived with the aroma of coffee. Sheena had gotten up without him knowing. He went to the bathroom, brushed his teeth, and washed his face before heading to the kitchen.

"Good morning."

She was fully dressed except for shoes. She was sock-footed, and wore a pair of blue jeans and a cotton baby blue blouse. "Please, Sheena. Don't cook for me."

She laughed, "I've been practicing. I'm really good at it now. Besides, you don't have anything here for me to cook. But you did have some rolls, so I put some in the toaster oven, so sit down and let me get you one."

Jason sat at the kitchen table and fantasized, as he did many times before, that they were married and that this was how they spent a lazy Saturday morning.

She put a plate of rolls on the table along with some butter. Then, poured him a cup of coffee and sat down with him at the table. "You need anything more?"

Jason smiled as he reached for a roll. "I need to know why you came here," he said as he picked up the butter knife.

"I needed to talk to you. I haven't seen you since before the accident and I've really missed you."

"They wouldn't let me see you."

"I know. My mother told me. Ivy told me what happened too." There was a moment of silence. She didn't know how to say what was needed to be said.

"I was told you're dating Marshall."

Sheena nodded her confirmation.

"What is it that you want, Sheena? What made you want to come here to see me after all this time?"

Sheena pulled an envelope from her jean's pocket. "I didn't get this until the day before yesterday."

He looked at the envelope he'd left at her apartment over a month ago. "What do you mean you just got it yesterday?"

"The person you gave it to took a two-week vacation, and even after he came back, it sat in a desk drawer until the day before yesterday because he'd forgotten about it."

"He promised me he'd give it to you. I paid him a hundred dollars."

"You would have done better by sending it express mail. But to answer your question, I remembered what we said to each other the last time we talked. I know we were to go our separate ways, but I just can't seem to stop thinking about the fact that we aren't on speaking terms."

"Yeah, but you're dating Marshall."

"And, you have a girlfriend... Brenda, right?"

Jason stared at her not saying one word.

"Anyway, what does that have to do with us being on speaking terms?

Jason was still silent.

They stared at each other for a moment. Then Sheena dropped her gaze to the floor. "Forgive me, it was really a bad idea to show up here unannounced." She stood with all intentions of getting her bag and leaving.

He stopped her by placing his hand on her arm. "Sit down. Let's talk this out." Sheena complied. "I left that note because I realized that I love you too much to allow our religious beliefs to separate us. I've tried to move on with my life and my heart just won't cooperate. But, if you still love me, we can work this out."

Sheena closed her eyes tightly after he made his last statement. She had not known how much she wanted to hear him say that until he did. But what was she going to do? Vincent was in her life now. "I told Vincent that I was coming here to put our friendship back intact." She was choked up with unexpected emotions that she had no clue how to handle. "But when I saw you last night and we hugged, I told myself that I didn't care about you being Muslim or me being Christian. All I cared about was the desire I felt for you at that moment."

"Sheena..."

"I don't want to hurt Vincent. I really care about him, but I'm not in love with him and he's not in love with me. But he's proposed and I wanted to resolve things between us before I give him an answer."

Jason tilted his head to one side, "All I've ever wanted was to be with you. I wanted to build a life with you, and the only reason why we haven't is because of you," Jason said flatly. "For years I waited for you. I was patient. Now after dating Vincent Marshall for less than six months, you are considering a marriage proposal from him?"

"You don't understand…"

"What don't I understand? I was brought up Muslim, Sheena, not an alien."

"Yes, I know you're right… I… please…. just tell me…. I mean… is it serious between you and Brenda, or any other woman for that matter?"

A slight frown creased his face. "If you're asking if I'd stop seeing her for you, then the answer is yes, in a heart beat. If you're asking if I'm in love with her or any other woman, the answer is, no."

Her brow furrowed.

"What's wrong?"

"What about our faiths. I have no intention on renouncing Jesus as my Savior."

"I told you before, I can marry a Christian. That's not a problem for me. The question is, are you willing to marry a Muslim?"

"I want to marry who I love."

He tilted h his head to the side trying to compute her meaning. Was she really saying she wanted to marry him, or did his ears just deceive him? He stood coming to where she sat and positioned his body directly in front of her. "Are you saying you want to be with me?" He needed confirmation.

"Yes," she sighed breathlessly. "But only if…"

In one smooth move Jason pulled her to him and kissed her with all the passion he had built up for her over the years. When finally their lips parted, he gasped, "I want to make love to you."

"Jason, we can't," she answered weakly.

"I need you, baby." Jason lifted her into his arms, carrying her to his bed, and gently placing her in the center.

Sheena's lips slightly parted as she exhaled an agonizing breath after he kissed her again. He was rendering her powerless by kissing her eyes, her ears, and her neck. He kissed her mouth again, this time savoring the taste of her tongue.

Sheena knew she should stop right now, but she had denied herself too long. She wanted him probably more than he wanted her.

*Oh God, forgive me, s*he prayed silently.

The battle was on in her mind, *stop him, don't do it, you know this is wrong.* His hot mouth seared her bare belly, "Ooh…" *Girl you're thirty-one years old, let it go.* He had caused her to be disoriented. Her concentration was on the passion surging through every part of her body.

Jason stopped long enough to pull her blouse over her head tossing it onto the floor and then his own. For Sheena, that was just enough time for her to come to her senses. "Jason, we can't," she gasped for air.

He stopped moving and gazed into her eyes. "Yes, we can. I've got to have you, baby."

The phone rang, but Jason continued to stare at her begging her with his eyes for permission to continue.

"The phone," she said to him.

She then noticed his labored breathing and his moisture-beaded head. "Please, baby, let me make love to you."

"Answer your phone."

He snatched the receiver from its cradle and barked, "Hello!"

Sheena could hear the woman on the other end. "I'm outside your house. I just knocked and you didn't answer."

"Look, Brenda. I told you I would call you."

"Open the door, Jason. I want to know what's going on."

God had made a way of escape and Sheena seized the opportunity. She moved from the bed, retrieved her blouse from the floor and went to the bathroom.

She looked at herself in the mirror and whispered, "thank you Lord," as she slid her blouse back on. The Lord had heard her cry and rescued her.

Her mind went to Marshall. He has been so wonderful to her and for her. He was her unofficial therapist, her light in darkness, and her friend. *It's just emotions,* her mind reasoned. *He had your hormones raging out of control, girl.* Ashamed of herself, she turned from the mirror and shut her eyes tightly.

Loud banging startled her, forcing her out of the bathroom to find out what was going on.

"Stay here, I'll be right back." Jason went to the front door.

"Let me in, Jason," She heard a woman's voice say loudly.

"No, I don't think so," he answered. "Go home."

"Open the door. I need to talk to you," she hollered.

"Talk to her, Jason." Sheena came up behind him. "I'll wait in your room." She walked away as Brenda continued to bang on the door.

Jason opened the door, but stood in the way so she couldn't enter. "Let me in, Jason," she whined.

Jason stared at her. "What did I tell you last night?"

"You've had all night to talk to her. And why is she still here?"

"Go home, Brenda. You and I will talk later," Jason said sternly.

"I want to talk now, and I want to talk to her."

Jason stepped out of the house, moved onto the landing, and closed the door behind him. "I've always been honest with you about my feelings for her."

"But you said it was over. You said she was out of your life."

"Yes, I said that and at the time, I thought it was over between us. But we're talking now and I'm certainly not going to allow you to ruin my chance to make things right between us. So, get your behind in your car and leave my house."

"No, I'm going to talk to her. I'm telling her everything."

Jason's nose flared, "Get away from here right now, or I promise you, I will call the police and have you arrested for trespassing. Now, think I'm playing if you want to," he said between clinched teeth.

Jason had never used that tone of voice with her and she knew he was angry just from the way he was staring at her. Brenda moved from the landing, got in her car, and started the engine. Jason went back into his house without watching her drive away.

Sheena was fully dressed with bag in hand when Jason entered the house. "What are you doing?"

"It's best that I check into a hotel. I really don't want to be involved in this type of drama. It was wrong of me to come here unannounced and cause problems with you and your girlfriend."

He walked towards her and took the bag from her hand. "She's not my girlfriend, not in the sense that you're referring to."

"Jason, she's clearly upset and she has every right to be."

"It would be no her at all if you and I hadn't agreed to that silly agreement to not speak to each other." Jason opened the coat closet and tossed her bag in.

"She's hurt, Jason."

"I never lied to her. She knew about you. She knows I'm in love with you." Jason pulled Sheena into his arms. "I just never imagined you would come to me and now that you did, I'm not letting you go. I love you too much. And right now, I want to finish what we started before we were so rudely interrupted."

Just as Jason was about to place a kiss on her lips, Sheena pushed him away from her. "It's a good thing we were disturbed, because we were about to enter the point of no return." She stepped to the window and watched as his girlfriend pulled out of his driveway.

"Oh, believe me, when I'm finished with you, you'll wonder why you hadn't entered that point sooner." He started toward her again.

"No, Jason," she said sternly.

"I need you," he said softly.

"You don't need me. You want me and to be totally honest, I want you too."

"Then come on, let's do this." He pulled her to him again.

"No, we're going to do what's right. We have a lot to talk about. We have issues between us that need to be resolved." She pulled away from him again. "Take me to breakfast. I need real food. I'm hungry. And, bring your bowling ball."

"Why does it always have to be your way?"

"It's not my way. It was my way before your girlfriend interrupted us. Now we need to do this the right way. God's way, it's even your Allah's way."

Jason stared at her for a minute and she stared right back at him. "I need to take a cold shower, so I'm able to put my pants on."

She looked at him unsympathetically, "do what you have to do."

Chapter Eighteen

Sheena couldn't persuade Jason to take her to a hotel. He promised not to seduce her, so she agreed to stay. They had gone to breakfast, went shopping at the underground, gone bowling, and stopped to eat again. It had been a long day and for that time, both of them were happy with no thoughts of Brenda or Marshall.

When Jason turned onto his street, she saw Brenda's car in his driveway. "Oh, no," he murmured.

"She isn't violent is she?"

Jason looked over at Sheena. He knew she had to be concerned after what she'd been through. "To be honest, I don't know. This is a side of her I've never seen before."

"You need to talk to her."

"She needs to honor my request, that's what she needs to do. I told her I'd call the police and I mean that," he gripped the steering wheel. "I don't like this, she has you shook up."

"I'm all right. I can only imagine how she feels."

Jason pulled into the driveway next to her car and Brenda got out before he shut off his motor and came to the passenger side of the car. "I need to talk to you," she hollered to Sheena.

Sheena had never been a fighter. She certainly wasn't going to start over a man. But, she knew if this woman touched her, it was on. She watched as Jason immediately got out of the car and headed toward Brenda.

"I told you to leave my place, didn't I? But, you won't listen. Well now, I'm calling the police."

"I don't care, call them."

"Are you out of your mind?"

"Did you tell her? Did you tell her everything?" Brenda asked while pointing at Sheena.

"She knows I love her. She knows you and I were … and I do mean were… seeing each other."

"So that's the way it is?" She was clearly taken back by the word *were*.

There was no reply.

"What about me, Jason. What about me?"

"Look, I'm sorry about everything. But, you did know I was still in love with her. I feel bad about all this. I never intended to hurt you," Jason said.

"So, it's over between us?"

Jason nodded. "I'm sorry."

"Can we just talk about this? Come home with me and let's talk about this."

"Things have changed. I'm not going home with you."

"Why Jason? You said all she's ever done was make a fool of you. Why are you allowing her to step right back into your life like this? What is it that she has over you?"

"I love her. I told you how I feel about her. I've never lied to you about how I feel about her. Look, I'm not going to keep going on and on about this."

"Please, don't do this to me," Brenda said brokenly.

"Move, Brenda," Jason commanded.

"No, not until I'm able to talk some sense into you."

"What do you want from me?"

"I want you to love me, Jason. I've been here when you were depressed and feeling low all because she put you down. It was me loving you through all that or have you forgotten? Why would you allow her to have access to your heart again? What is wrong with you?"

"You don't understand. You never understood how I could lay in bed with you and call out her name."

Sheena shut her eyes tightly and whispered to herself, "That was cruel, Jason."

"But, you said it was over. You asked me to give you time to get over her. You can't do that by allowing her to walk in and out of your life when she feels like it," Brenda tried to reason.

"You always knew my feelings for her were still here," Jason pointed to his chest.

"So, it only took an appearance from her to rekindle the relationship."

"She's all I ever wanted."

"So, I don't stand a chance?"

"I love her. I can't help that."

"She's making a mockery of you and you're letting her."

"We'll see about that."

"Will I have to take you to court for child support?"

Jason stared at her.

Brenda turned and sternly looked at Sheena. "Know this, you'll be dealing with me for the rest of your life and I promise you, I'm going to do my best to make your relationship with him a living hell." She turned, got into her car, and pulled out of the driveway, wheels squelching as she sped off.

Sheena was stunned. Jason opened the car door and Sheena didn't move.

"I was going to tell you about that."

Sheena gave him a deadly look, "When?"

"I don't know when."

"Maybe you can give me a round about, before or after the wedding?" She asked between clinched teeth.

"Let's go into the house."

Sheena saw Jason's neighbor looking on, so she complied.

Soon after the front door was shut, Jason turned to her and said, "I hate that you found out that way?"

"Yeah, me too. You should have told me. You should have said something immediately. Why would you even take her through this when she's the mother of your child? What kind of man are you?"

"That was an accident."

"Accident? God doesn't make accidents, Jason."

"How long have you known?"

"A few weeks now."

"Did you know when you left me that note?"

"No." Sheena stared at him as if she didn't believe him. "I swear to you. When I left the note she hadn't told me she was pregnant."

"I need to talk to her."

"No, you don't."

"Yes, I do. I need to apologize to her. I was wrong for coming here."

"No, you weren't."

Sheena paused to think. "I came here on a whim and that was wrong. Now, I've not only screwed up my life, but an unborn child's life in the process."

"Baby, listen to me. I will take care of that child. I would never turn my back on my own flesh and blood."

"That's good to know. Now, what you need to do is work things out with her."

"What?"

"You heard me." Sheena went to the closet to retrieve her bag.

"Don't do this, Sheena."

"I'm doing what's right. When you and her conceived that child, it wasn't about you or me or her anymore."

"Don't do this, baby," Jason pleaded.

Sheena had her cell phone to her ear. "Yes, can you please send a cab to…"

"Don't do this…" He listened as she gave the address and ended with…

"Please come right away." She closed the phone. "I want to apologize to her. Will you give me her cell number?"

Jason stared at her long and hard just before he walked away.

"Jason…"

He slammed his bedroom door.

ಲಿಂ

Sheena was back in Philadelphia in her bed staring up at the ceiling. She had been trying to fall asleep, but she had been in bed two hours and it was four in the morning and sleep had not come.

During that time, she had decided not to marry Jason or Marshall. How could she marry a man she did not love, or a man who was expecting a child by another woman?

Why hadn't she just left well enough alone? She and Vincent were getting closer, and now she'd ruined even that. What had she done in her life to deserve this? She balled in a fetal position and before she could stop herself, she cried out loudly.

ಲಿಂ

The Sunday morning sun peeped through Sheena's bedroom window. Normally, she would have been up, preparing to go to church, but she was not going today. She laid in bed the whole morning surfing the channels looking for nothing in particular. Each time the phone rang, she looked at the Caller I.D. Jason had called her five times before noon. On Monday, she did the same thing - laid around all day.

On Tuesday evening Sheena's mother used her key and came into her apartment. She called her name as she entered.

"I'm in the bathroom."

She found her relaxing in the tub with bubbles up to her neck. "You haven't answered your phone. You've got everyone worried about you."

"I'm sorry. I was going to call you tonight."

"What's going on?"

"Nothing, I just needed some time to regroup that's all."

"The prosecutor's office called me. What's his name... uh, Randall. He said that that woman who attacked you is under psychological evaluation and will probably be there for a while."

"I figured as much."

Her mother closed the lid on the toilet and sat on it. "What happened in Atlanta?"

"Nothing I want to talk about."

"Jason's been calling everyone. He told me to let you know he'll be here Friday morning."

"Jason and I have nothing to talk about. But thanks for telling me. I'll be sure not to be here when he comes."

"Did you forget about the revival this week?"

"I sure did."

"Well, we all promised Mother Evans we'd support her program. So, are you coming tonight?"

"No."

"Sheena, baby.... What's going on with you? And before you say nothing, I want you to know I talked to Jason."

"Did he tell you he's going to be a father?"

Her mother was silent.

"Oh, he didn't tell you that did he?"

"No, he said that you left upset and that he was concerned about you."

Sheena slid deeper into the water shutting her eyes tightly forcing herself not to cry.

"I told you to leave that man alone. I begged you not to go."

"I'm glad I went. Now I know it's truly over," she said brokenly.

"Well, then I'm glad you went. Now you can get him totally out of your system and press forward. Who knows, maybe you and Vincent will have a chance to..."

"I'm not going to see Vincent anymore."

"Why? What has Vincent done to you?"

"He's done nothing. I'm a walking disaster and I don't want to screw up his life along with my own. Besides, he's looking for a wife and I'm never marrying. Ever!"

"You're hurting right now. You're saying that because of the pain you feel."

"I'm saying what's in my heart." A tear escaped her lid.

"Look, your father and I will be here around six to pick you up for church tonight. The Prophetess that's speaking is an awesome woman of God."

"I'm not going to church tonight."

"Then, we'll pick you up tomorrow?"

"No, I'm not going tomorrow."

"Thursday?"

"No day," she said firmly.

Sheena's mother stood abruptly. "Mother Evans has planned this event for over a year. You promised to support her. I expect you to attend one day at the least."

"I'm giving church a rest for a while."

"A rest?"

"What's wrong with you? Have you totally lost your mind? 'Cause it sure seems to me that you have. You don't let a man allow you to lose your relationship with the Lord. 'Cause without God, you are nothing, do you hear me?"

"I'm nothing with God, Mommy. Look at me. I'm almost thirty-two, by the time you were my age you had a family. What do I have?"

"God is all you need to get what you want and what you need."

"Yeah, well, I've done it God's way and where has it left me - alone that's where. I'm all alone." Sheena raised herself from the tub, snatched up her towel wrapping it around her, and walked past her mother into her bedroom with her mother following behind her. "I'm going to do things my way now. I'm going to do what I want, when I want, and how I want. There's crack heads out there living a more abundant life than I am."

"What does it profit a man to gain the world and lose his own soul?"

"I don't know, but I'm going to find out."

The phone rang and Sheena's mother stared at her as she turned to go into her closet. "Are you going to answer that?"

"I don't feel like talking to anyone."

"Divide and conquer," her mother whispered as she understood what the enemy was doing to her child. She answered her phone. "Hello."

"Hi, is Sheena available?"

"May I ask who's calling?"

"Vincent Marshall."

"Oh, this is Christina, Sheena's mother."

"Hello Mrs. Daniels. Is she all right? I've been calling her since yesterday and she hasn't returned my calls."

"She's fine. I came here because she wouldn't answer any of my calls either."

"Can I talk to her?

"Hold on and let me see if she'll take the phone. Sheena, Marshall wants to speak with you."

"Tell him I'll call him later."

"Marshall."

"I heard her."

ಬಂಗ

By Thursday Sheena still had not left her house, but she did however, talk to Ivy who practically begged her to come to the revival. So far, Sheena had been a no show. Marshall had only called one more time, leaving one message, *if you need to talk, I'm here for you.*

Later that evening after hearing Marshall's message, Sheena stood at his front door in the pouring rain knowing that now was the time to get back into her car and drive home, before she actually carried out what she plotted in her mind to do. But, she was a woman on a mission. For once in her life, she was going to do what she wanted to do. She was tired of being alone, tired of feeling unfulfilled, and her plan was to do something about it. She had never been in Marshall's house even though she had come here with him a few times. She had never gone in. She knocked on the door and rung the door bell.

She knew he was entertaining guests because there were several cars in the driveway. It came to her again to get back into her car and go home, and just when she was about to do just that, Marshall opened the door with a surprised look on his face, "Sheena!"

She tried to speak, but not one word would form. Then, she broke into tears clasping into his arms. Marshall guided her into the house and up the stairs to his bedroom. Sheena tried to take control of the wave of emotions that seemed to overcome her, but her efforts failed.

"What's wrong, baby?"

"I don't want to be alone, I...."

"It's all right. I'm here for you. Look, I have guests in the living room and I didn't think you wanted them to see you this way, that's why I brought you up here." He sat on the bed next to her.

Sheena nodded her understanding. "Thank you."

"What's going on? What's made you so upset?"

Sheena had all intentions of telling him she was sorry for interrupting his evening and she would leave. But before she could speak, Marshall noticed she was shivering and rubbed her arms. "You're wet. You need to take these clothes off." Marshall immediately moved to his closet to get her something dry to put on. "Here," he handed her an oversized t-shirt. "Go into the bathroom and take off those wet things. I'll put your clothes in the dryer." When she didn't move right away, he encouraged her, "go on, before you catch a cold."

Sheena went into the bathroom and did what she was told. Just before leaving, she looked at herself in the mirror and knew after this night, she'd never be the same.

Marshall stood at the bathroom door waiting for her to come out. He took the wet clothes from her hand, walked over to his bed, and pulled back the spread. Come here, he patted the bed beckoning her to come to him. She sat and he swung her legs onto the bed. I have guests that I need to get rid of. You relax and rest while I'm gone. I promise not to be too long, okay?

Sheena only nodded.

Marshall pulled the sheet over her body. Relax, you're safe with me. He kissed her on the forehead.

Sheena finally spoke, "I'm sorry, I shouldn't have come here without notice. I knew better than this."

No, it's okay. I'm glad you felt like you could come to me. I'll be back shortly. He picked up the television remote and clicked on a channel. Here, watch some T.V. Then he disappeared.

Sheena looked over at the clock on the nightstand. It read 8:37 PM. The battle in her mind began, *get your behind out of that man's bed and take your fresh tail home.* But Sheena ignored the warning, fixed her eyes on the movie playing on television, and drifted off to sleep.

When Sheena opened her eyes, she was staring into Marshall's. "Hey, you fell asleep."

"I'm sorry," she sat up.

He smiled, "No, I'm sorry. I shouldn't have awakened you." Marshall moved to the chair in the corner of the room and Sheena followed him with her eyes. "Your clothes are all dry." They are folded on the chair.

She noticed that he had removed his shoes and unbuttoned his shirt showing his t-shirt. Again every instinct commanded her to get her stuff and leave.

Marshall sat next to her on the bed. "You ready to talk about what's bothering you?"

"Not right now. I just didn't want to be alone tonight."

"Okay, go on back to sleep. I'll sleep in the guest room right across the hall, so just call me if you need me."

Sheena nodded her head and watched him as she moved toward the dresser taking out some things and leaving the room.

Sheena lay in the bed wide awake contemplating what to do. After reasoning with herself for about a half hour, she got out of bed and walked across the hall to where Marshall was. His door was not closed and she could see him on the top of the spread in only a pajama bottom. "Vincent," she called from the door.

He turned his head toward her, "What's wrong? Can't you sleep?"

Sheena never answered him. She walked up to his bed. "I need you," she said brokenly.

Marshall was a little alarmed. "I'm here for you, baby." Marshall got out of the bed, took her by the hand, and led her back into the other room.

"I don't want to be alone," she complained as he pulled the sheet over her body for the second time.

"Okay, I'll stay in here with you until you go to sleep."

"Will you lay with me?"

"I don't think that's a good idea."

"Please," she said breathlessly.

Against his better judgment, Marshall stretch out next to Sheena and she laid her head on his chest. After a moment he asked, "are you comfortable?"

"Yes."

"Good, now go to sleep." She may be comfortable, but he sure wasn't. He had no idea how he was going to make it through the night.

She raised her leg across his and ran her hand over his stomach and there it rested. As soon as she fell asleep, he was going back across the hall.

They lay there just like that for about fifteen minutes. Then, out of nowhere, Sheena whispered, "make love to me, Vincent."

Maybe he was hearing things. He knew that's what he wanted to do, but there was no way this woman would allow that to happen. He didn't move a muscle.

Sheena sat up in the bed and pulled the t-shirt over her head.

"What are you doing?" He said with alarm in his voice.

"Make love to me, Vincent. Please," she pleaded softly.

"Baby, no. You're vulnerable right now. You'll hate me in the morning."

"No, I won't. Please."

Marshall shook his head. "No, it's not right. Sheena, I know you. You're under a lot of stress and I don't want you to make a decision you're going to regret." He got out of the bed, picked up the t-shirt she disrobed, and attempted to put it back on her.

"No!" Sheena got out of the bed. "You don't have to make an excuse. Just say you don't want me." She went to the chair where her clothes were folded, gathered them up, and headed to the bathroom.

"That's not it at all." Marshall was standing in front of the door preventing her from getting in. "How many times have you told me sex without marriage was out of the question?

"I've changed my mind."

"Baby, look at me. I've wanted you ever since we shared our first kiss."

"Then make love to me. Now."

Marshall hesitated. "Are you sure?"

"I'm begging you and you're asking me if I'm sure."

He took the clothes from her hand dropping them to the floor.

ಏಁಃ

Marshall woke up about seven that morning. He noticed Sheena was not in bed. He called out her name thinking maybe she was in the bathroom or even downstairs. He called for her again and still no answer. Looking around the room he saw that her clothes were gone and the t-shirt he'd given her to wear was neatly draped across the back of the chair. He picked up his phone to dial her number. The machine picked up. Then he dialed her cell phone getting the message center. "Sheena, why did you leave without waking me? Call me." He placed the phone on the base.

Marshall ran his hand over his head wondering why she left him without saying anything. He picked up the phone again this time calling his office letting them know he would be late this morning. It was Friday and he didn't have anything important going on anyway. What he decided to do was to get dressed and talk to Sheena.

After showering and dressing, Marshall decided to put fresh linen on his bed and when he removed the blanket and top sheet, there on the fitted sheet was the evidence of Sheena's lost virginity. He blew out a long sigh. He needed to talk to her now more than ever.

Chapter Nineteen

Sheena had avoided Marshall all day. He had told her once morning came she would regret her decision and he was right, she did. Nevertheless, she couldn't blame him. He gave her what she asked for. No, what she begged for. Though she had repented from her heart and soul, it hardly seemed good enough.

With trepidation, she called Ivy.

"Where have you been all day. I've been calling you since nine this morning," Ivy said as soon as she heard Sheena's voice.

"I've been in prayer most of the day," she answered honestly.

"Well, I can't be mad at cha' for that. Anyway, Marshall's called me three times today. He thought maybe I had heard from you."

"Oh," was her only comment.

Ivy was silent for a moment. "What's wrong, Sheena? You don't sound right."

Sheena blew out a long sigh. "I messed up, Ivy. I messed up royally."

"We all screw up sometimes, so what ever it is, don't beat yourself up over it."

"No, you don't understand. I really messed up," Sheena whined.

Ivy heard the urgency in her voice and paused giving her space to talk, but when the silence stretched between them Ivy said, "your mother told me you went to Atlanta over the weekend. And ever since you came back, you've been held up in your apartment not communicating with anybody. Now, I don't know what happened while you were there, but what ever it is, you know God is a forgiving God. Admit it, quit it, and forget it. I don't know of anything that God won't forgive you for other than blaspheming against the Holy Ghost."

"Well, it's not as bad as blaspheming."

"See then, you'll be all right. Just be grateful God allowed you to live through your sin to repent," Ivy said with a slight chuckle.

"I'm serious, Ivy."

"So am I. Now tell me, what did you do?"

"I'm really not ready to talk about it right now."

"Well then, keep it to yourself. Too much information is dangerous anyway. Especially since you think I judge people."

Sheena had to giggle, not making any comment to her statement. "So, what are you doing this evening?"

"I'm going to be in the church house, girl. Why haven't you been? All of us promised Mother Evans we'd been there."

"I haven't been up to it."

"Well this is the last night and you really need to show your face since you did tell Mother you'd support her.

"My mother said the minister is really good."

"I've never seen anyone like this woman before in my life. She preaches, teaches, and prophesies. I think the woman has five of the nine gifts of the spirit."

"Really?"

"Girl, the woman is a true prophetess. She called me to the front of the church on Tuesday night and told me stuff I never even shared with God. She's awesome. This is the last night, you know."

"Yes, I know."

"I'll tell you what. I'll come and get you so you won't have to drive. Hold on, let me get the other line."

It wasn't long before Ivy was back, "That's Marshall on the line. I told him I was talking to you and he told me to tell you he was on his way to your apartment."

"Tell him not to come and that I'll call him later."

Ivy hesitated, "Okay, hold on."

"Ivy," she called before she clicked back to the other line.

"Yeah."

"I'm going to hang up, but I'll be ready at six."

"Okay, I'll see you then."

Ivy and Miranda picked Sheena up precisely at six that evening. All the way to the church, Ivy and Miranda testified how awesome Prophetess Debra Lewis was. So Sheena's expectations for a magnificent service grew, and when she walked into the church, she came in looking for a blessing.

Ivy had told her that during the five-day revival that started on Monday night, the church was only half full. But, the people who had come out on Monday came back on Tuesday bringing others and by Friday, Cathedral of Faith was standing room only.

Now the service was just about over and Sheena was disappointed that the prophetess had not called her out as she had done so many others. She wanted confirmation and answers to questions she had been praying about for a long time. But now the service had come to an end with the benediction moments away, and Sheena was leaving unfulfilled.

Sheena watched as the Prophetess went back into the pulpit and stood at the podium to thank Mother Evans and Pastor Jones for inviting her. Then she gave accolades' to the church staff for treating her like royalty all week long.

Prophetess Lewis asked the church to stand to their feet, but as she raised her hand to give the benediction, she hesitated and stared into the crowd. "I'm going to ask everyone to sit back down," she scanned the church with her eyes. "I need an usher. Come quickly."

Sister Perry, who is a retired nurse, came to stand before her. Then Prophetess Lewis looked to her left and after studying the faces of the people, she announced with authority, "the Devil is a liar." Then she looked to her right. She smiled at Sister Perry and said, "I want you to go to the seventh row and then I want you to have the twelfth person sitting in that pew to stand."

There was a moment of confusion because there was a child that lay sleeping on the pew next to Miranda. So when the usher asked the man next to Sheena to stand, it was Miranda that pointed to the child who had not been counted.

By this time the Prophetess had made her way to the floor. "It's not a man, it's a woman. The Lord said count the people on the pew. Then she looked directly at Sheena and said, "you know it's you."

Sheena slowly rose to her feet.

The Prophetess began pacing the floor. After a few moments she suddenly stopped, turned in Sheena's direction and said, "God blocked it, it wasn't him and it wasn't her. God is the one that blocked it. Do you understand?"

Sheena nodded.

"God blocked it, because He has something better for you. But you failed to see the blessing because you've been distracted. What God has for you will bring you the joy and the peace missing in your life.

Genesis the second chapter, verse eight says, *And the LORD God said, It is not good that the man should be alone; I will make him an help meet for him.* It's God who makes that choice, not you. Do you understand?"

Sheena nodded.

She turned to the congregation and said, listen to me people, when God gives you a mate, it's a done deal."

Echoes of amen was heard throughout the Church.

"What God joins together, only death will separate it."

More echoes of amen and that's right was heard.

She directed her attention back to Sheena. "What God has chosen for you will stand through the test of time because it's been ordained by Him," she pointed upward.

She looked at the congregation again. "The problem with us is we like to do what moves us now. What thrills us now, but God looks past the first six months, he looks, past a year, he looks past ten years, and centuries, right into eternity."

"Amen," Pastor Jones said loudly.

She looked to Sheena again, "you made a few decisions without consulting the Lord. Now, you're paying the price."

Tears began to fall from Sheena's lids as she nodded.

"Help her up here, please." The Prophetess paused a moment before speaking again while the usher helped her to the front of the church. "You were raised in the ways of our Lord and for years no matter the trial or tribulation, you stood fast to his Word... Uh..., until lately, and you understand don't you?"

Sheena nodded trying her best to keep her composure.

"Don't you doubt the Lord or His love for you. It was Him who gave the permission to test you. You've been guarding yourself against the wiles of the enemy for years. And He is well pleased with you. And no matter what you've been thinking, his love is able to cover all your transgressions, and all your pain, all of your sorrow, and yes, even your wavering faith. Why? Because He loves you more than you love yourself."

"Satan has used a multitude of tactics on you. He's been messing with your mind, keeping you confused about...." She stopped mid sentence. Sheena was totally overwhelmed by the words of the prophetess. "Ooh, I see... that's how you made some of the decisions you have.

At this point, Sheena nearly doubled over seemingly in pain, gasping as her lungs contracted for air. Now the tears fell on their own fruition.

The Prophetess stood back as if she was surprised to see Sheena's reaction.

"You wanted me to call you out. You wanted to see if I was a true Prophet of God. But I understand.... You've seen a few phonies in your lifetime. But you now know the words I speak come from the Father."

Sheena nodded, smiling and crying all at the same time.

"The Bible says, *But if they cannot contain, let them marry: for it is better to marry than to burn.* Do you understand?"

Sheena nodded.

"You need to be filled. You've been living this life without total protection for far too long. It's time for you to receive the baptism of the Holy Ghost. Would you like to be filled?"

Sheena nodded, "yes."

"Good. God is about to perform an operation on you. But when he finishes with you tonight, you're going to have a better understanding about a lot of things, and most of the questions you've petitioned God for will be answered. He's about to equip you with His anointing so you'll have staying power. Oh my God, who is the woman here that's close to her that's been called to the ministry?

Miranda stood.

"Come her sweetie, come quickly."

Miranda ran to the front of the church, "You don't have to worry about her anymore, she'll be..."

The Prophetess stopped mid sentence. "Oh my God... bear with me people...." She began to pace the floor. "Your beauty has been a tremendous burden to you. I'm sure I don't have to elaborate on that."

"Sheena dropped her head to the floor."

"You've even been ashamed of being so attractive. You've hidden behind sunglasses and you won't wear make-up, you've always tried to down play your looks. Hold your head up and don't be ashamed of how God made you. It's God that give you favor in the sight of all them that look at you."

Sheena lifted her head and looked directly at her.

"Let me tell you about another extra ordinary beautiful woman named Esther. Beauty caused Esther to be chosen by the king to be his wife. The bible says that *Esther obtained favor in the sight of all them that looked upon her* and because of her beauty, she was able to say, If I parish I'll parish but I'm going to see the king. She was able to save a nation of people. Read Esther 2:15. As a matter of fact read the whole book of Esther." She glared at Sheena for a moment then said, "You didn't know that your beauty was designed for a similar purpose?"

Sheena looked at her perplexed.

"It may not have been a nation of people, but important, nonetheless.

Sheena still did not understand where the prophetess was going.

"There are men in this very church who started coming as teenagers just because you were a member. But once they sat in these pews and heard the Pastor preach the Word of God, the Word penetrated their heart and they were saved. You didn't know that did you?

Sheena was still mystified, "no."

The prophetess looked over at Pastor Jones. "Did you know that Pastor?"

"Yes, I have confirmation of a few."

"Well, there's more than a few. The ones you know of were the ones that confessed that they started coming for the wrong reason and stayed for the right reason."

You could hear amen throughout the church.

"You've been seeing someone that you've just begun to trust."

Sheena stared back at the Prophetess. Then she murmured the answer.

The Prophetess whispered something to Miranda then she walked toward the back of the church until she got to the last pew where Vincent Marshall was sitting. After whispering something to him, they came to the front of the church and stood before the Prophetess.

The Prophetess did not speak right away. She paced the front of the church for a minute. At first Marshall stood with his hands clasped behind his back. But it tore at his heart to see that Sheena was crying. He took her hand.

She looked at Marshall. "You don't belong to this church, do you?"

"No," he answered with a strong voice.

"But you come sometimes?"

"Yes."

"When did you start coming?"

Marshall gestured toward Sheena, "When we started dating."

"Where do you go when you don't come here?"

He gave the Prophetess a slight smile. "Nowhere."

She looked at Sheena. "See what I mean."

Sheena looked over at Marshall smiling and he returned one of his own.

"You can close the book on that old mission. Now there is a new mission that's been placed on you. You're going to be dealing with a lot of young people. Many will come to you lost and you'll give them direction through the Word. You may not understand right now, but you will. You're going to be a great advocate for a lot of confused people.

Sheena nodded.

The Prophetess stood directly in front of Sheena and Marshall. "I need a strong man to stand behind him," she said to the men sitting on the front pew. Then she looked at Miranda. "You stand behind her," referring to Sheena. Then the prophetess began to pray for both of them and near the end of the prayer she lifted her hands to touch their heads and both of them fell under the anointing of the Holy Ghost.

ಌಓ

"In my whole life, I've never seen nothing like it," Sheena heard Pastor Jones say as she began to come to herself. "…and I've been in the ministry all my life."

"Listen, Daddy. She stopped speaking in tongues."

"The Prophetess said let her wake on her own," she heard Pastor Jones answer.

"It's just amazing to me how God works. I would have never believed that Vincent Marshall would be laid out in nobody's church unless it was his own funeral?"

"Yeah, but he was back on his feet within five minutes."

"Yeah, but his butt was still slain by the Spirit," Miranda answered.

Sheena opened her eyes.

"Welcome back to earth," Miranda greeted first.

"I passed out?"

"Girl the Holy Ghost knocked you off your feet."

Sheena tried to get up, but her head was spinning and her body felt weak.

"Don't try to get up right away. You were speaking in tongues for over twenty minutes," Pastor Jones said. "Even the Prophetess said she'd never seen anything like it before. She said God never used her like that before."

"Sheena started laughing."

"What's so funny?"

"She looked around the room and just laughed and for the life of her she did not know why. All she knew was she felt good all over and joy was all over her. The laughter was infectious and the chain reaction started with Pastor Jones bursting out in laughter, then Miranda, Ivy, and finally Mother Evans. They laughed and couldn't stop themselves. The laughed until it hurt.

Marshall was sitting in the north entry of the church waiting for Sheena. He had no intentions on coming to church tonight, but when Sheena did not return his calls he showed up knowing Ivy was bring her here.

The benediction had been given over an hour ago and they were still in the Pastor's study.

Marshall's thoughts went back to the events of the evening. Though he only came to church to get a chance to talk to Sheena, he realized God had something else in store for him and it had been mind blowing. He believed in prophets, he just never thought he would actually meet a real one. After he raised himself off of the floor, the Prophetess told him that his whole life was in the middle of a transition and he would never be the same.

He knew that to be the truth, because ever since he had given Sheena the envelope asking her to marry him, his life hasn't been the same. He had known since that day that he was deeply in love with her. He just hadn't told her. He had wanted to say it last night, but he did not want her to think that the words were being said out of lust. It was nobody but God who spoke to him after the prophetess walked away from him saying, *don't wait, marry her quickly.*

Marshall turned his head toward the laughter. He stood as Mother Evans, Ivy, and Miranda came up to with Sheena leaning on Miranda for support.

"Are you able to drive baby?" Mother Evans asked Marshall between giggles.

"Yes." Marshall looked at them with a puzzled look on his face."

"Good. Here." Miranda moved Sheena towards him placing her hand in his. "She's so drunk in the spirit; she's got us drunk too."

"Take her straight home, Marshall," Ivy said. Make sure she's settled in before you leave her. Come on, we'll help get her in the car."

"What is so funny?" Marshall wanted to know.

"We'll explain another time," Mother Evans answered.

They were still laughing when they left the sanctuary.

Chapter Twenty

The telephone woke Sheena the next morning from a good night's rest, "Hello."

"Can we talk now?"

"Jason?"

"I've gotten everything straight between me and Brenda."

Sheena pulled herself up to lean on the headboard of the bed, "that's good. I'm really glad things are working out between you two."

"I want you to marry me, Sheena."

"I can't do that," she answered without hesitation.

"Why? I love you and you love me. I just told you I straightened out that other situation and…"

"I'm marrying Vincent."

"What?"

"I'm marrying Vincent," she repeated.

"No, Sheena, you can't do that. I need you. Why are you doing this?"

"Jason, just listen to me for a second."

"I don't want to hear that you're marrying Vincent Marshall."

"Well, that's the way it is."

"I'm in Philly. I'm coming to your house."

"No, I don't want you here."

Marshall appeared at Sheena's bedroom door.

"I'm on my way there, we need to talk…"

"I don't want you to come here, please Jason."

Marshall walked up to Sheena's bed, "give me the phone," he ordered. "Jason... Jason," he called trying to get his attention.

Sheena watched Marshall as he sat on the side of her bed.

"Jason, this is Marshall. Do all of us a favor. Don't call my fiancée anymore."

"Jason.... look buddy... it's over okay. What you thought you had with her is over. She belongs to me, okay."

Sheena could hear Jason talking but she could not make out what he was saying to Marshall.

"I understand all that, and I feel for you. But she's marrying me, and that's all there is to say."

Marshall paused again to listen to what Jason had to say.

"Look, man, I don't need to see you and Sheena don't need to see you. She told you she's marrying me, and I'm confirming what she's told you. That's it. She's mine and I'm not about to give her to you. I don't care how much you have invested." Marshall paused, "well, I'm in love with her too."

Sheena was surprised to hear him say that.

"Now, please, do us all a favor and stay away from my woman." Marshall ended the call.

"I'm not a piece of property," Sheena pouted.

"I know. I was just trying to make him understand that you're going to be my wife, not his."

"What are you doing here?"

"Well, when I placed you on your bed last night, I didn't go home. For one, I was too tired to drive and for two, I really didn't want to leave you."

Sheena smiled at him. "Did you sleep in the other bedroom?"

"Yes."

"Were you comfortable?"
"Very."
"Good."
"So you mean what you said, right? You're marrying me?"

She smiled at him. "Yes, I meant what I said."

Marshall looked up at the ceiling, "Thank you, God." Then he leaned towards her and kissed her passionately on the lips.

Sheena ended the kiss and with a serious look in her eyes, "We can't let what happened the other night…"

He stopped her words by placing his finger on her lips, "you don't have to say anything. Nothing else will happen until we're married, I promise."

She knew he would understand.

"I was thinking. We learned a lot last night wouldn't you say?"

"I know for me a lot of things were confirmed."

"I remember us talking about your purpose for being here. Do you remember that?"

"Yes."

"Is that clear to you now?"

"Crystal."

"Want to share your purpose with me?"

Sheena gave him a shy smile, "Well, Jade asked me to talk to a teen that attends her tutoring program who confided in her about being confused about his sexuality. When she asked me to talk to him, I didn't even think about it, I simply turned down the opportunity to help because I didn't think I was qualified to even talk to him. Besides, I didn't want anyone to know I struggled in that area."

"And now?"

"Now, I don't care who knows. Maybe my testimony can help someone else. So, I'm going to let Jade know

I've changed my mind and I'm going to talk to the young man."

"I think you'd be a good youth counselor."

"I'll need training."

"So, get some training."

Sheena looked into his eyes, "Did you mean what you said?"

Marshall looked straight back into her eyes and said, "I try never to say anything I don't mean."

"So, you meant what you said when you told Jason that you loved me?"

"Oh, yes, I especially meant that," Marshall said as he moved from the bed heading for the door. "Get dressed. I'm going to get you no less than a carat to put on your finger."

Sheena smiled. "Jewelry shopping, yes," she shouted in triumph!

Marshall threw back his head and bellowed in laughter and happiness!

Epilogue

More Than A Year Later

"Randi wanted a huge wedding and she got exactly what she wanted," Ivy said as she watched Miranda throw the bouquet into the crowd of women who leaped high trying to catch it.

"It must be five hundred people in this ballroom," Jade commented.

"Randi said Kyle's mother sent out the most. If I'm not mistaking I think she said the woman had five hundred people on just her list alone," Ivy added.

"Well, all I can say is the food is superb," Sheena picked up a shrimp from her plate and dipped it in cocktail sauce. "The crab cakes are cooked to perfection. Where is my husband?" She looked out into the crowd. "I want him to get me some more of them."

"Where in the world are you putting all that food? You're going to be sick." Jade laughed loudly. "You do know that's your second plate, don't you?"

"Oh, you're monitoring me, Jade?"

Between chuckles Jade continued, "No, I'm just trying to warn you. No, it's not you I should be warning, it's Marshall I need to caution. He's the one who'll have to play nurse, because you ate too much."

"Leave her alone," Ivy whispered to Jade. Then she raised her voice so Sheena could hear her over the noisy ballroom. "Eat all you want," she touched Sheena's extended belly. "You're eight months pregnant and it's only been in the last month that your appetite has picked up. So leave her alone, Jade."

Sheena smiled at her friend, "Thanks, Ivy."

"I was just thinking, this is the third wedding in less than two years," Jade recognized.

"It sure is," Ivy agreed. "You celebrated your first year back in February. Sheena you celebrated your first just last week and I'm celebrating my first anniversary next week."

"If my anniversary wasn't so far off we could celebrate together," Jade said.

"We can still celebrate together," Sheena added.

"Yeah, I guess we could."

Marshall, Darrell and Bill came over where the women were sitting.

"Where did you all go?" Ivy asked.

"Oh, we had to decorate Kyle's car."

"Tell me you didn't do it with condoms, please tell me you didn't."

"Kyle did it to me," Marshall said with a smirk on his face. "It took us a half hour to remove those things, remember?" He looked to Bill.

"It sure did."

"And I had to remove them because Sheena didn't want to drive all the way up into the mountains with condoms all over the car."

"Payback," Darrell said giving Marshall a high five.

"And you of all people, Darrell. You're a minister of the gospel."

"What does that have to do with anything? We're just having some clean fun. Besides, they're married now, so I'd say it's decent and in order, Miss Ivy."

"You have a point," she agreed.

"Vincent, can you get me another crab cake?" Sheena asked her husband.

Marshall stood to his feet, "Sure baby."

"She's going to be sick, Marshall." Jade said laughing.

"That's all right, I'll doctor her back to health," Marshall said walking away.

Sheena licked her tongue at Jade, "Now, ha!"

"You have really become a big baby," Jade stated.

"Randi's mother really looks nice," Bill said.

"She does look good. I think this is the most I've seen her smile in a long time."

"She's hardly used that oxygen tank today, Sheena added."

"Yeah, she was determined to stand and give her child away without that thing in tow," Ivy stated.

"I'm just glad she lived long enough to see this day," Sheena remarked.

"It's truly something anyone will not soon forget," Bill added.

"Daddy is trying to get your attention, Darrell," Ivy observed.

"I'll be right back," Darrell said to his wife.

"I'll be back, too. I'm going over there and speak to the Mothers of Cathedral," Jade said walking away as Marshall approached the table.

"Your crab cakes, baby," Marshall sat next to his wife.

"Thanks," she caressed his face.

"Don't stay here and tire yourself out," he whispered to his wife.

Sheena was serious when she said, "You worry about me too much. I'm fine, honey."

"Can't I be a little extra concerned about you in your delicate condition?"

Sheena thought about his comment a moment. "Come here," she said beckoning him with her finger.

"What?"
"I love you," she softly whispered in his ear.
"And I love you."

Three weeks later…..

Sheena had been in labor for eighteen hours with Marshall by her side when finally Amari Dakota Marshall came into the world kicking and screaming at the top of her lungs, weighing in at six pounds and eleven ounces.

Ivy, Miranda and Jade all claimed to be the baby's godmother.

Dear Reader:

I hope **SHEENA'S DILLEMMA: It's Better To Marry Than To Burn** has answered all the questions that have been building since the start of this series.

I have truly enjoyed writing each dilemma even though Sheena's personality was the most challenging. There were a lot of things about her characteristics I just didn't agree with, and to be honest I tried to change them as I began line editing this story. I guess that's why I lost *my version* of this manuscript twice, once because my computer crashed and the other because it was accidentally written over by another file.

As I began to rewrite this story, I knew it was not going to follow the traditional Christian fiction established by the industry. Especially since I used the name Jesus, but nobody come to the Father unless it's through his son, Christ Jesus. So in the end, God's will was done and the Holy Ghost made an appearance.

I'm still getting email about Pastor Preston Owens and it is my prayer that God will give me a story to tell. I'm itching to write Jason's story. I think that would be interesting.

As always, I love hearing from readers. So, drop me a line and tell me what you think about the series and if you would like to see it continued.

Until next time, may God continue to bless and keep you, this is my prayer.

Peace,

Reign
P.O. Box 4731
Rocky Mount, NC 27803-0731

On the Web: www.Reign.NickiAngela.net
Reign@NickiAngela.net

The Dilemma's Series by Reign
Book #1   Book #2

The Dilemma's Series are stories based around Ivy Jones-Miller, Sheena Daniels, Miranda Jones, and Jade Sanders. Each woman tackles trials and tribulations and wins against all odds through their faith in God and love and their love and devotion of friendship. Books In The Dilemma Series: "Ivy's Dilemma (Thy Will Be Done)" published 2005 and "Jade's Dilemma (Lead Us Not Into Temptation)" published 2006.

Call toll free: 1-877-209-5200 to order by phone or use this coupon to order by mail.

Name_____

Address_____

City_____ State_____ Zip_____

Please send me the books I have checked below.

      ___**Ivy's Dilemma – Thy Will Be Done**
         $12.00 USA $19.00 CAN

      ___**Jade's Dilemma – Lead Us Not Into Temptation**
         $12.00 USA $19.00 CAN

        I am enclosing $_____
    Plus postage & handling $_____
      Total amount enclosed $_____

*Add $1.65 for the first book and $.60 for each additional book. Send Money Order. (No Cash, C.O.D. or Personal Checks) to Dreams Publishing Co. P.O. Box 4731, Rocky Mount, NC 27801.

All In The Family
By: Janice Sims, Melanie Schuster & Maxine Thompson
ISBN-13: 9780977093663

The Johnson sisters haven't been home to tiny Mason Corners, South Carolina for a long time. Their mother, Sara, feeling neglected, gives them an ultimatum: Come to the family reunion...OR ELSE!!!

In **Best Selling Author, Janice Sims's MOMMA'S BABY, DADDY'S MAYBE**, perfect wife and mother, Candace, 41, of Charleston, has to come to terms with the nasty paternity rumors that have been making the rounds in the family since she was a child. Angela, 25, a super-model wannabe in Miami wants to come home, but what will the man she left behind do when she tells him what she had to do to survive while they were apart?

In WHERE MY HEART IS Melanie Schuster gives us a glimpse into the life of Sharon, an A-personality, 32 year old successful New York City television producer who has excelled at everything she's ever tried. What drives her to always be on top? In striving for perfection, has she missed the signals her handsome co-worker has been sending for two years now? She finds out when she asks him to pose as her man at the family reunion.

And in **Maxine Thompson's SUMMER OF SALVATION** Debra, 35, a casting director in Hollywood brings her Mexican-American husband home for the first time. They eloped. Will Debra and her mother have a showdown during the festivities? Whatever happens at the Johnson Family Reunion, you know that it will be kept... "All In The Family."